# H♥TBED H♥TEL

*AN AMERICAN FARCE*

by

**Michael Parker**

# SAMUEL FRENCH

FOUNDED 1830

SAMUELFRENCH.COM

## IMPORTANT BILLING AND CREDIT
## REQUIREMENTS

All producers *of HOTBED HOTEL must* give credit to the Author of the Play in all programs distributed in connection with performances of the Play, and in all instances in which the title of the Play appears for the purposes of advertising, publicizing or otherwise exploiting the Play and /or a production. The name of the Author *must* appear on a separate line on which no other name appears, immediately following the title and *must* appear in size of type not less than fifty percent of the size of the title type.

# HOTBED HOTEL

First produced at the Delray Beach Playhouse, Delray Beach, Florida, on October 15th, 1992, with the following cast:

| | |
|---|---|
| HOPKINS | Jack Gordon |
| TERRI CODY | Nedria DeGrotta |
| BRIAN CODY | Michael DeGrotta |
| MAJOR PONSENBY | Michael Parker |
| MAUREEN | Darrah Devereaux |
| SAM LEWIS | Marc Streeter |
| ASHLEY | Pamela Schreck |
| HAYLEY HARRINGTON | Susan Barnes |
| DOROTHY | Carolyn Gordon |

Directed by Randolph DelLago

Designed by Ann Caderet

The action of the play takes place in The Turtle Beach Hotel in the Florida Keys.

Time: The Present

Act 1     An afternoon in January
Act II    Scene 1: The action is continuous
            Scene 2: Later the same evening

# CHARACTERS

HOPKINS (Age 50 – 60): The hotel handyman. He is an endearing comic character who continually surprises the audience by producing, throughout the play, bottle after bottle of liquor which he has hidden all over the stage. He guarantees his life-long employment by never fixing anything permanently and is at the heart of most of the visual comic sequences.
A natural comic, usually tipsy, occasionally drunk.

TERRI CODY (Age 30 – 40): While her husband Brian calls himself the hotel manager, it is very apparent that she runs the place. She clearly has to love him very much to be able to put up with his blunders, inefficiencies and disasters. While she is the brains behind the Hotbed Hotel façade, she remains a gentle, loving, loyal wife.
Smart, efficient, competent yet tender and patient.

BRIAN CODY (age 35 – 40): The hotel owner and manager, he is one of life's hopeless incompetents. Meaning well and trying hard, without a mean bone in his body, he somehow always manages to end up with a disaster on his hands. He is not dominated by his wife, but it is just his great good fortune that she is always there to make any decision that needs to be made for him. He is one of life's dreamers who wanders through every day with little understanding of what is going on around him.
Kind, helpful, understanding, naïve.

MAJOR PONSENBY (Age 50+): A product of an almost by-gone age, that of the upper class British military officer. He is a total eccentric, but nevertheless a real character who, while changing back and forth into the role of his twin brother, creates hilarious diversions from the main plot, culminating in an extraordinary *coup-de-theatre* at the final curtain.
As Major Ponsenby: Eccentric (to say the least) but with a sparkling dry wit and sense of humor.
As Abdul El Hajj: Serious, dour and taciturn.

MAUREEN (Age 18 – 25): The hotel maid. She really doesn't have a brain in her head. However, she is always bright and cheery, always tries very hard and should appear like a ray of sunshine every time she steps onto the stage.

Young, sexy, pretty, full of energy.

SAM LEWIS (Age 40 – 60): A New York business man, full of flash, bravado and moral judgment. It is not until the arrival of his wife, late in the play, that we realize he is, in fact, staying in the hotel with his girlfriend. A different Sam then emerges, a fawning, hen-pecked husband, completely dominated by Mrs. Lewis.

Brash, loud, a moral hypocrite.

ASHLEY (Age 30 – 45): Sam Lewis' girlfriend is glamorous, sexy and a real "looker." Through no fault of her own, her clothes keep disappearing throughout the play. As she wanders in and out wearing only a towel, she is hardly aware of the bedlam going on around her.

Gorgeous, but not cheap or tawdry, with a kind, affectionate nature.

HAYLEY HARRINGTON (Age 30 – 45): Also known as "The Barracuda" for her aggressive attitude towards men. She is glamorous and sensuous. Her reputation as a predator has preceded her. Focusing on one male after another, sometimes in a lighthearted, almost frivolous way, she does not let the audience down. (If Terri is responsible for the Hotbed of intrigue in the Hotel, Hayley is responsible for the literal Hot Bed.)

Voluptuous, sexy, a determined nymphomaniac.

DOROTHY (Age 45 – 60): Although it is late in the play when, to the total surprise of the audience, she is introduced as Sam's real wife, her character of "the old battleaxe" completely dominates the final twenty minutes. After a loose screw in the number of her hotel room door, 6, is dislodged causing it to flip down and become 9 (the Barracuda's room) and she is visited by all Hayley's paramours, she is at the heart of one of the great comic sequences of the play.

Severe, matronly, self-opinionated

# ACT I

*(The curtain rises on an empty set. It is the reception area, hallway and room 7 of The Turtle Beach Hotel. Situated in the Florida Keys, it has been converted from an old mansion into a small but functional hotel.*

*The hallway D.R. leads to the bar, dining room and front entrance of the hotel. R. is the reception area with a double-hinged door leading to the office. The reception area has clearly been adapted from a corner of the old house and is rather cramped and cluttered. The wall has key racks, booking charts, etc., and there is a call bell and telephone on the counter. U.R. is a staircase [See Author's Note.] with a landing facing the audience. D.R.C. are two low backed easy chairs, a small coffee table and a stand-up ash tray.*

*U.C. and U.L. are the doors to rooms 6 and 8, their numbers large enough to be seen by the audience. On the wall between rooms 6 and 8 are two paintings. The one on the R. is hinged with a recess behind it. The one on the L. is a still life with a bottle of wine as part of the subject matter. [See Author's Note.] In the center of the hall, slightly L. of the door of room 6, is a hanging light fixture [See Author's Note.] U.L., the hallway leads to other rooms, laundry, etc.*

*The L. side of the stage consists of room 7, its number clearly visible when the door is open, with its rear wall cut away immediately R. of the door frame. There is a "do not disturb" sign hanging on the inside doorknob. U.L. is the door to the dressing room and D. L. the bathroom. Extreme D.L. would be French doors, but one is cut away leaving only one, opening onto the garden patio. The room contains a double bed and two bedside tables with a phone on the L. one. There is a vase of flowers on a small semi-circular table against the wall L. between the dressing room and the bathroom doors. The bedspread is a light floral design and the room is delineated with a carpet.*

*After a few moments HOPKINS enters the hallway from U.L. He is easily identifiable as a hotel handyman. He wears scruffy white overalls, T-shirt and baseball cap. He has a variety of tools slung on his belt. Age perhaps 50-60. He has definitely seen better days. The ravages of time and alcohol have clearly taken their toll. He is, however, a friendly soul who wouldn't be happy if he didn't have something to complain about.*

*He comes R., looks up the stairs, peeks in the office door, comes D. R. and has a quick look towards the front entrance. Seeing no one, he quickly retreats to the picture hanging on the wall between rooms 6 and 8. He reaches into a recess behind the R. picture and produces a bottle of liquor from which he takes a long drink as the phone in the reception area rings. He hurries to put the cap back on the bottle, replaces it in its hiding place and exits U. L. as TERRI comes downstairs to answer the phone.*

*She is an attractive woman age 30 to 40, very business-like in her manner and quietly efficient in everything she does. She is dressed in a light-weight cotton skirt and blouse.)*

TERRI. *(Calling as she appears at the top of the stairs.)* Brian. Brian. Now where's he gone? *(Sighs.)* I only asked him to watch the phone for fifteen minutes. *(Picks up phone.)* Turtle Beach Hotel. May I help you? — I'm afraid the manager *(She rolls her eyes heavenward.)* is out. I'm his wife, Mrs. Cody, could I help you? — When? — Next Saturday, one double? We are very busy, could you hold on a minute while I check. *(She places her hand over the speaker and silently counts to ten.)* We're very lucky sir. I see we have a cancellation, we can definitely fit you in. — Good. — The name is? *(Writing on a small pad.)* — Right, I've got that, and that's Saturday the 17th. One double for three nights. I'm sure you'll enjoy it sir. Thank you. *(She hangs up.)* Well that doubles our occupancy rate!

*(Enter BRIAN from the front entrance. He is middle aged, rather nondescript looking, always nervous, and seems to be perpetually on the edge of panic as though he can barely cope with life. He is not dominated by TERRI but he simply prefers to leave all major decisions to her. He is wearing cotton pants and a short-sleeve*

*tropical shirt. He is limping, wearing one shoe and holding the other out in front of him at arms length.)*

BRIAN. That damn dog next door!

*(He comes upstage to the entrance to the reception area and pauses.)*

TERRI. How do you know it's the dog next door?

BRIAN. Because he always does it in the same place.

TERRI. If he always does it in the same place, why do you step in it dear?

BRIAN. *(Looks blank.)* Why do I —?

TERRI. Never mind. Where were you anyway? I asked you to watch the phone.

BRIAN. Well. Nobody called so I went down to the beach.

TERRI. Oh Brian, you're hopeless. Why don't you leave your shoes outside the front door?

BRIAN. I can't do that. Leave *(Holds out shoe.)* this? For people to see. Really! This is a first class hotel.

TERRI. Oh? Has it changed hands while I was upstairs?

BRIAN. *(Limping into office.)* You know what I mean. What would the guests think?

TERRI. Guests? We've only got one, and I don't believe he's capable of thought.

*(She is busy with the booking chart. BRIAN comes back in, now minus both shoes.)*

BRIAN. I don't think you should make rude remarks about the Major. At least he pays his bills.

TERRI. Yes, I will say that for him.

BRIAN. You know, he's not short of money. The other day he showed me a painting he'd just bought for seven hundred dollars.

TERRI. Good God. Seven hundred dollars? And you can't even wear it.

BRIAN. Anyway, he's not a guest. He's — well — he's a permanent resident.

TERRI. Well, I know that dear, but why a retired British army officer would stay in this hotel for nearly two years, I can't imagine. I don't believe he's all there.

BRIAN. What do you mean, you don't think he's all there?

TERRI. Well, you know, his elevator stops — *(She holds her hand across her neck.)*

BRIAN. I don't know at all. He's led a very interesting life. You'd be surprised at some of the places the Brits find to send people. He lived all over the world before he retired.

TERRI. Oh Brian, you can't believe all his ridiculous stories. You know as well as I do, he's as nutty as a fruitcake.

BRIAN. I'm not so sure — speak of the devil. Good afternoon Major.

*(MAJOR PONSENBY has entered from U. L. and comes R. toward the foot of the stairs. Age, perhaps 50. A tall, straight gentlemen dressed very smartly in well-pressed pants and a semi-military short-sleeve white shirt with pockets and epaulettes.)*

MAJOR. Good afternoon Brian. How are you today?

BRIAN. Just fine, thank you Major.

MAJOR. Ah — The fair and beautiful Mrs. Cody. How are you my dear?

TERRI. I'm fine, thank you Major.

MAJOR. Good. Good. If you don't mind my saying so, you look very beautiful today.

TERRI. Well thank you Major.

MAJOR. Did I ever tell you that sometimes you remind me very much of my dear old mother.

TERRI. Really?

MAJOR. You're not as sad as she was though.

TERRI. Sad?

MAJOR. Yes. All her life she seemed sad. On account of my brother I suppose.

BRIAN. What happened to your brother?

MAJOR. I've no idea.

BRIAN. What?

MAJOR. We never knew. It was very sad. My twin brother, and I never saw him.

TERRI. How can you have a twin brother that you've never seen?

MAJOR. Well, you see he was gone before I was born.

TERRI. What?

MAJOR. Yes. You see Mother was married to this nomadic North African Sheik and all he wanted was a son. As soon as my brother was born he packed up his tents, took the baby and abandoned Mother to the desert. He never knew she was carrying twins. Two hours later, I arrived. Later that day we were saved by a wandering caravan. Very romantic in a way.

TERRI. Well, you certainly can tell a tale Major. Why — you almost had me going then.

MAJOR. Yes, quite. *(Seeing BRIAN in his socks.)* I say old chap, joining the barefoot brigade are we? Reminds me of the time I was in Buano Buano. Lost me boots in the quicksand, spent 42 days —

TERRI. *(Can't stand another of the MAJOR'S stories.)* I'm sure that's very interesting Major, but I have to — er — go and get Brian some shoes. *(She heads upstairs then turns.)* And Brian?

BRIAN. Yes dear?

TERRI. Stay by the phone.

*(TERRI exits upstairs.)*

BRIAN. Oh! Right.

MAJOR. She's got you on duty, eh?

BRIAN. Well, she doesn't want to miss any calls.

MAJOR. Quite right. Quite right. Must keep the lines of communication open. Reminds me of the time General Sinclair sent a runner 31 miles across the desert. That was in Booticapa you know.

BRIAN. Where's that?

MAJOR. What? Booticapa? Africa old chap, sort of — er — in the middle.

BRIAN. What was it like?

MAJOR. Well now. Let me think. How would you describe Booticapa? Lets put it this way, if the world needed an enema, Booticapa is where you would insert the tube!

BRIAN. Well, either there or Miami Beach!

MAJOR. Ah, very good old chap, very good. *(He pauses.)* You know Brian, I'm very happy here at Turtle Beach.

BRIAN. And we're happy to have you Major. You do know we're trying to sell the place don't you?

MAJOR. Well, I'd heard rumors. May I ask why?

BRIAN. Well, what you probably don't know is that this hotel is run as a nonprofit organization.

MAJOR. I say, that's damned noble of you old boy.

BRIAN. No-no-no. We didn't intend it to be. It just worked out that way.

MAJOR. Oh, I see.

BRIAN. The fact is that it's almost impossible to make money with a twelve-room hotel. We haven't got the capital to expand so we have to sell it to someone who has.

TERRI. *(Entering down the stairs with a pair of BRIAN'S shoes in her hand.)* Are you still here Major?

MAJOR. No, I left a couple of minutes ago.

TERRI. *(Ignoring his response.)* Mr. Cody has things to do you know. He can't stand around chatting all day. Here you are dear. *(She hands BRIAN his shoes.)*

MAJOR. Very well madam. I can take a hint. I know when my presence is no longer required. There's no need to say any more. May I remind you that my family motto is "NIHILGENDO E PLANITUS SANCTIVITUS ENIM IMPEDIMENTO".

BRIAN. Good heavens. What does that mean?

MAJOR. No one's ever known really! Have a nice day.

*(He exits jauntily to the front entrance.)*

TERRI. *(Laughing.)* I'm going to miss him when we sell this place.

BRIAN. Talking of selling, where do we stand with that right now?

TERRI. We appear to be down to one good prospect. That Mr. Lewis from New York, and he's supposed to be coming down in a week or two.

BRIAN. I suppose we really do have to sell, huh?

TERRI. Yes we do. We've never made a nickel out of this place, and in the eight years we've owned it the land value has absolutely shot up. We can make a fortune by selling it. Well, a small one anyway.

BRIAN. I do wish we didn't have to sell it. Money doesn't buy everything you know.

TERRI. I know that. That's why I have credit cards. Anyway, we can barely make the payroll, and apart from the dining room, we've only got two employees. A maid and a handyman.

BRIAN. Well, we're supposed to have a gardener as well. If I could only find one.

TERRI. That reminds me. What happened to that young boy who applied last week?

BRIAN. Oh, he wasn't any good.

TERRI. What was wrong with him?

BRIAN. He said he wanted to start at the top, so I sent him into the garden to dig a hole. An hour later he quit.

TERRI. Oh, that reminds me. I meant to tell you. Hopkins might be drinking again, so I'm keeping the bar locked during the day. I've put beer, wine and soft drinks in the fridge in the office. Incidentally, did you get Hopkins to fix that running toilet in number seven?

BRIAN. *(Very proud.)* I didn't need to. I fixed it myself.

TERRI. *(After the longest pause.)* You what?

BRIAN. I fixed it myself.

*(TERRI stares at him for a moment unable to believe her ears, then turns, goes up the hall and calls off U. L.)*

TERRI. Hopkins! *(She enters room 7, goes to bathroom, opens door and looks in. We hear water running, she turns to the audience, rolls her eyes to the heavens, comes out of room 7, then back R. to reception area.)* Cody, Find Hopkins!

BRIAN. But dear—

TERRI. Find Hopkins!

BRIAN. Well I —

*(BRIAN hurries out of the front entrance. TERRI opens the door of*

*room 6, looks in, then goes to room 8, looks in.)*

TERRI. Maureen, would you get a bucket and mop please, quickly. *(TERRI heads R. to the reception room as MAUREEN comes out of room 8 and quickly disappears U.L. MAUREEN is very young, very pretty and, as we shall see, not too bright. She is wearing very short shorts, T-shirt and no shoes. Enter HOPKINS from the front entrance.)* Ah, Hopkins. We have a disaster in room 7.

*(TERRI goes back into room 7 followed by HOPKINS. She leads him to the bathroom. He looks in.)*

HOPKINS. Has Mr. Cody been fixing things again?
TERRI. I'm afraid so.
HOPKINS. I ought to get hazardous work pay, with him living in the place.
TERRI. Can you fix it?
HOPKINS. I dunno. Looks like he might have cracked the bowl. Anyway, I'm not paid to get my feet wet. I'll go and turn the water off and get my tools. You'd better do something about all that water.

*(HOPKINS exits out of room 7 and U. L. as MAUREEN enters with a bucket and mop.)*

TERRI. Thank you Maureen. Could you please try to mop up all this water. Hopkins'll be back in a minute to fix the toilet.

*(TERRI exits out of room 7, R. to reception and up the stairs.)*

MAUREEN. Yes ma'am. *(She starts to mop, and has just bent forward in the bathroom doorway, her derriere in full view of the audience , as HOPKINS enters room 7, a toolbox in one hand and a plunger in the other. He steps forward with the plunger in his outstretched arm, close to MAUREEN'S derriere, then stops and thinks better of it as MAUREEN turns and sees him.)* What are you staring at?
HOPKINS. Well — er — I — er — If they got any shorter, you'd

have two more cheeks to powder.

MAUREEN. *(Laughing.)* You're a dirty old man.

HOPKINS. Old? Yes, I suppose I am. They say the first thing that goes is your memory. Well, I forgot I'm not supposed to enjoy looking at a pretty girl *(MAUREEN giggles.)* How are you doing there?

MAUREEN. Are you kidding? I only just got started.

HOPKINS. Right. Might as well make myself comfortable then. *(Singing softly to himself, he goes to the door, takes the "Do Not Disturb" sign off the inside doorknob, places it on the outside, closes and locks the door. He then puts his toolbox on the bed, opens it and takes out a whiskey glass. He breathes into it, polishes it with his handkerchief, then produces a thermos out of which he tips ice cubes into the glass. He then pauses and looks around the room.)* Now. Lets see. Room 7. Ah, yes! *(He moves to the flower vase on the table between the dressing room and the bathroom doors, lifts out the flowers with one hand, reaches in with the other and produces a bottle of liquor. He pours a generous shot into the glass, replaces the bottle and the flowers, returns to the bed, takes out a small red and white checkered cloth from his toolbox, spreads it on the bed, sits up with his feet on the cloth and sips his drink.)* It's a hard life!

MAUREEN. I noticed. *(She continues to mop.)* What'll you do if they sell this place?

HOPKINS. Oh, I guess I'll stay here. The place would fall apart without me.

MAUREEN. You know I noticed that. There always seems to be something going wrong.

HOPKINS. That's my pension plan.

MAUREEN. What?

HOPKINS. My pension plan. The secret is never fix anything permanently.

MAUREEN. One of these days they're going to catch on. What's that you're drinking anyway?

HOPKINS. Oh, you wouldn't know.

MAUREEN. You'd be surprised what I know.

HOPKINS. As a matter of fact, it's a nice Polish vodka. It's what the Pope drinks.

MAUREEN. Yeah? That's probably why they have to carry him

everywhere! *(Picks up the bucket.)* Well, that's about it. It's pretty dry now.

    HOPKINS. *(Getting off the bed and packing up his tool box.)* O.K., I'll see you later. *(He watches wistfully as MAUREEN unlocks the door and exits U. L. He flexes his hands like a pianist about to play.)* Here comes the genius of the John!

*(He picks up his toolbox and plunger, exits into the bathroom and closes the door as the phone in the reception area rings. BRIAN rushes in from the front entrance, sprints around the counter and picks up the phone, just as TERRI appears at the head of the stairs. He grins at her and she retreats.)*

    BRIAN. Turtle Beach Hotel — Yes — Yes — What? Mr. Lewis — today — half an hour ago — well, I suppose so. O.K. Bye. *(He hangs up and starts running in sheer panic, all over the place.)* Terri, Terri, quick, Oh my God what are we going to do? *(TERRI comes quickly downstairs.)* The place is a mess, we've got a hole in the front yard, the hotel is empty, he'll never buy it. We'll be poor for the rest of our lives. Everything's gone wrong and that damn dog's done it again out front. *(Sees TERRI.)* Terri, what do you think?

    TERRI. I think compared to you, Murphy was an optimist. What is it?

    BRIAN. Mr. Lewis from New York, — you know, the guy who's interested in buying this place — his secretary called. He flew into Miami this morning. He's driving down and he should be here about four o'clock.

    TERRI. I see. *(Looks at her watch.)* Well, at least that gives us a little time, but not much.

    BRIAN. What are we going to do? How are we going to sell a hotel, when we've only got one guest in the middle of the season?

*(Enter the MAJOR from the front entrance.)*

    MAJOR. Is everything alright old chap? I heard shouting.
    TERRI. *(Taking charge.)* Yes, everything is going to be fine.
    BRIAN. Fine! How can you say that? How can we sell an empty hotel?

TERRI. Because it is not going to be empty. I've got an idea. We're going to create some guests. Major, do me a favor will you? See if you can find Maureen for me, and bring her back here. Brian, would you please get Hopkins. He's in the bathroom in number 7. *(Exit MAJOR U.L. BRIAN goes into room 7 and into the bathroom. He reappears with HOPKINS who carries his toolbox and plunger.)* Now — if I remember correctly.... *(She looks at the booking chart on the wall.)* Ah-ha. Oh dear. Not her! Well, beggars can't be choosers. *(The MAJOR comes R. with MAUREEN and they all stand around the reception area, except BRIAN who slumps dejectedly into one of the chairs.)* Now, pay attention everyone. As you've no doubt heard, Mr. Cody and I are trying to sell the hotel, and we need you all to help us.

MAUREEN. Why should we help?

HOPKINS. Yeah. Why should we help you put us out of work?

TERRI. Because if we don't sell it, we'll probably have to close the hotel, and you really will be out of work. But if we do sell it, you'll all be getting big fat bonuses, and who knows, maybe you'll be able to work for the new owner.

HOPKINS. That makes sense. Alright then. We're with you Mrs. C.

MAUREEN. That's right.

MAJOR. Jolly good show.

TERRI. Listen everyone. A Mr. Lewis, from New York, is arriving this afternoon and we need to create the right impression. We're going to convince him that this is a busy, prosperous hotel.

HOPKINS. This I've got to hear.

BRIAN. Well, we are a one star hotel you know.

MAJOR. Jolly good show. How good is that?

HOPKINS. Well let's put it this way, there's no such thing as a no-star hotel!

TERRI. Now. Here's what we're going to do. Brian, you're going to be on your own in charge of everything.

BRIAN. Where are you going to be?

TERRI. I'm going to be shopping in Miami.

BRIAN. *(He leaps up, starting to panic again.)* Oh great! That's just great! That's wonderful. That's typical, just like every women in the world. When the chips are down, you go shopping. You're going to leave me to —

MAJOR. Steady on old chap. Don't panic.

BRIAN. What else is there to do? You heard her, she —

TERRI. Brian! For heavens sake. I won't really be in Miami. You'll just tell Mr. Lewis I am.

BRIAN. I will?

TERRI. Yes.

BRIAN. Why?

TERRI. Because that way I can check into one of the rooms and pretend to be a guest. We're going to make him think the hotel is full.

HOPKINS. That's brilliant Mrs. C. You and the Major make two.

TERRI. I haven't finished yet. You're going to be a guest too, Hopkins.

HOPKINS. Me?

TERRI. Certainly. All we have to do is get you out of those overalls, and into some casual clothes. I'm sure we can pass you as a distinguished and influential guest.

MAJOR. Jolly good show. Reminds me of the time —

TERRI. I'm sure we'd all like to hear about it Major, but some other time perhaps. We are in a bit of a hurry.

BRIAN. Well, now you've got three guests. That's hardly full, but I suppose it's better than one.

MAJOR. Wait a minute. Wait a minute. Can't I pretend to be someone?

BRIAN. You're already a guest Major.

MAJOR. Ah-yès. Quite right old chap, but couldn't I pretend to be another buyer and drive the price up?

BRIAN. That's one hell of an idea.

TERRI. No Major. I don't think so. You just be yourself. Now Maureen, you're going to do all the things I usually do. As well as maid and laundry, you're going to have to be receptionist and room service. You're going to have to spread yourself around.

MAUREEN. What's room service? I don't think I like the sound of servicing somebody in their room.

TERRI. I'll explain it all to you in a minute. You have nothing to worry about.

MAUREEN. I'm scared Mrs. Cody. I'll never remember what to say.

TERRI. Don't worry. I'll write it all down for you. Now about our fourth guest.

*(They all look at each other counting.)*

BRIAN. We've run out of people.
TERRI. No. I just checked the booking sheets. We have another guest checking in today. A real one.
BRIAN. Who?
TERRI. That's the problem. Hayley Harrington!

*(There is a long silence. MAUREEN looks blank, the others look knowingly at each other.)*

HOPKINS. Oh my God!
BRIAN. Anyone but her. She'll ruin everything.
MAUREEN. Who's Hayley Harrington?
MAJOR. The Barracuda!
MAUREEN. Who?
TERRI. Roboslut!
MAUREEN. Who?
TERRI. Let me explain, Maureen. Miss Harrington stays here every year, and while she's on vacation she — er — pursues her hobby.
MAUREEN. What's wrong with that?
TERRI. Her hobby is men!
MAUREEN. Men? I don't understand.
TERRI. You know how men in the old west used to cut notches on the handles of their guns? Well she collects men in much the same way, only she cuts notches on her bedpost. If you know what I mean.
HOPKINS. Well she's never tried to collect me.
MAUREEN. You mean she — in bed?
BRIAN. Let's put it this way. She lost her virginity a long time ago.
MAJOR. But she's still got the little box it came in!
MAUREEN. You mean she goes after men — all the time.
MAJOR. She's so used to being on her back she gets dizzy when she stands up.

BRIAN. Just like the Mounties, she always gets her man.

HOPKINS. Well she's never tried to get me.

MAUREEN. How long has she been coming here?

BRIAN. I dunno. Since before we bought the place eight years ago.

MAUREEN. It's a wonder there's anyone left.

HOPKINS. I'm left.

MAUREEN. How long have you known her Major?

MAJOR. *(Thoughtful.)* Well, when you say "known," do you mean in the biblical sense?

TERRI. Never mind that. The important thing is to keep her away from Mr. Lewis.

BRIAN. Never mind that, keep her away from me.

TERRI. I've got it! Major. You wanted to be a part of this. That'll be your job.

MAJOR. Jolly good show! What'll be my job?

TERRI. Keep the Barracuda away from Mr. Lewis.

MAJOR. How am I going to do that?

TERRI. *(Teasing.)* Oh, I'm sure you'll find a way.

MAJOR. Steady on old girl. I'm not sure I'm very good with aggressive women. I remember once the General's daughter, big strapping lass she was, had a mouth on her just like horse. Well, one day she got me on the billiard table, I think it was, and do you know in the heat of the battle I couldn't get my little soldier to salute!

TERRI. *(Laughing.)* I'm sure you'll do just fine Major.

MAJOR. I must say you appear to have put me in the front lines.

HOPKINS. That's right Major. You'd better get ready for the frontal assault. And if I know the Barracuda, probably a full frontal! I think you should put in for combat pay Major.

MAJOR. I'm not sure it's going to be that bad old chap, but I do seem to remember she can knock the fruit right off your loom if you're not careful.

TERRI. Come on you guys. Let's get going. Hopkins, is the bathroom in number 7 OK?

HOPKINS. Working like a charm, Mrs. C.

TERRI. Good. We want to put Mr. Lewis in there. It's our best room because it has that little dressing room. O.K. Lets get started.

Hopkins, Maureen, let's get upstairs so I can see what I can turn you into.

HOPKINS. I'll just put my tools away Mrs. C. and I'll be right up.

*(He exits U. L. as TERRI and MAUREEN head up the stairs. MAUREEN exits, TERRI stops and turns.)*

TERRI. Oh — and Brian?

BRIAN. Yes dear?

TERRI. Do you think you might be able to change that light bulb in the hall without blowing up every power station south of Atlanta?

BRIAN. Nothing to it my love.

TERRI. I know that. But do you think you can handle it?

BRIAN. Of course.

MAJOR. I'll lend a hand Mrs. Cody. Fear not. Combined Anglo-American forces will be brought to bear. Pressure will be exerted, armies will be mobilized, reserves will be brought up and the campaign will be fought to a successful conclusion.

TERRI. Why do I get the feeling this isn't going to work?

*(Exit TERRI upstairs.)*

BRIAN. O.K. You get the step ladder from the garage. I'll get a light bulb.

*(Exit BRIAN U. L. Exit MAJOR front entrance. Enter HOPKINS from U. L. He comes R. to the foot of the stairs, sees there is no one around, goes down to the front entrance, looks furtively outside and hurries back to the stand-up ash tray. He lifts off the top section, reaches in and produces a bottle of liquor from which he takes a long drink. He replaces the bottle and ash tray top and exits upstairs as the MAJOR enters from the front entrance carrying a step ladder, and BRIAN enters from U. L. with a light bulb. They meet in the middle of the hall.)*

MAJOR. *(Setting up the ladder under the light.)* Here we are old chap.

BRIAN. Major, would you make sure the switch is off please.
MAJOR. *(Goes to the foot of the stairs and looks.)* Right, it's off.
BRIAN. O.K. Up we go then. *(He climbs the ladder which the MAJOR holds.)* Now, let's see. Here, hold this Major. *(He hands down the bulb he has just unscrewed.)* Now what's this? It looks like a loose wire. Major, could you get me a small screwdriver please?
MAJOR. Right on, old chap.

*(The MAJOR exits out the front entrance. TERRI enters down the stairs. As she reaches the foot of the stairs, she flicks on the switch and, without breaking stride or looking up at BRIAN, exits U. L. BRIAN has been frozen in place. As soon as she is gone, his legs lose contact with the ladder and go straight out sideways almost doing the splits as he hangs by one hand. [See Author's Note.] TERRI returns almost immediately with a bundle of clothes over her arm.)*

TERRI. *(Walking straight past him with hardly a glance.)* Stop pretending to be Tarzan, Brian, and just change the bulb.

*(She turns off the switch and exits upstairs.)*

BRIAN. AEIOOOW!

*(BRIAN slumps back on the ladder. Enter MAJOR from the front entrance with a screwdriver in his hand.)*

MAJOR. I say, old chap, are you alright?
BRIAN. A-a-a-r-r-gh!
MAJOR. Your shorts too tight or something?
BRIAN. A-a-a-r-r-gh!
MAJOR. You really ought to take something for that you know.
BRIAN. A-a-a-r-r-gh!
MAJOR. You sound just like the mating call of the Nigerian Nymphomaniac Nambians. Did I ever tell you about the time —
BRIAN. Stop Major! This is no time to discuss the sexual habits of the Nambians whatever they are. I'm going to get this job done,

come hell or high water. Now, would you please pass me the screw-driver.

*(The MAJOR hands BRIAN the screwdriver. BRIAN, who still has the light bulb in one hand, now realizes that he needs both hands on the fixture. He pops the screw end of the light bulb in his mouth to hold it and reaches up with both hands. Enter MAUREEN from upstairs. She is now in her room service outfit. She wears a wig and is dressed in a black dress, white apron, hose and high heels. She carries more clothes on a hanger over one arm. She holds a number of 3 x 5 cards from which she is reading.)*

MAUREEN. Good morning sir or madam. Welcome to the Turtle Beach Hotel. I am your receptionist. I am here to be of service. Would you kindly complete this form. *(As she reaches the foot of the stairs she flicks on the light switch. The light bulb in BRIAN'S mouth now lights up as he goes totally rigid on the ladder. MAUREEN continues on behind the counter and hangs the extra clothes on the landing banister rail. The MAJOR, seeing BRIAN, rushes to turn off the switch and the bulb in BRIAN'S mouth goes off. The MAJOR returns to the ladder. MAUREEN flips to the next card.)* Good morning sir or madam. I am your room service waitress. Would you like to see the — er — er *(She squints at the card, goes over, switches on the light again.)* M.E.N.U. *(The light bulb in BRIAN'S mouth lights up again.)* What does M.E.N.U. spell?

*(The MAJOR rushes to the switch again and turns it off. The light bulb in BRIAN'S mouth goes off.)*

BRIAN. A-a-a-r-r-gh!
MAUREEN. I know. It's menu.
BRIAN. A-a-a-r-r-gh!
MAJOR. There it is again, you sure we don't have any Nigerian Nymphos in this hotel?
BRIAN. A-a-a-r-r-gh!

*(He slumps down, draped over the top of the ladder like a rag doll.*

*Enter SAM LEWIS from the front entrance. He could be any age from 40 to 60. Smartly dressed in a business suit and tie, he is carrying a suitcase. He is followed by ASHLEY. A "looker," she is voluptuous and a little flashy without appearing too cheap. She is dressed in a very smart light-weight summer suit, high heels, lots of jewelry, etc. She too carries a small suitcase.)*

ASHLEY. *(Looking around.)* Oh, Sam, it's just lovely.

SAM. Not bad. Not bad at all. *(He sees the MAJOR who has rushed D.R. to prevent them from seeing BRIAN.)* Good afternoon. My name is Lewis. *(He hands the MAJOR his card.)* I believe you're expecting me. Do you have my room ready?

MAJOR. Mr. Lewis? Room? Oh yes. Our receptionist Miss Maureen, will get you registered.

MAUREEN. *(Aside to the MAJOR.)* I'm not the receptionist. *(She indicates her dress.)* I'm room service.

MAJOR. Remember? Spread yourself around. You are the receptionist.

MAUREEN. But I've got my room service dress on.

MAJOR. Then you'll have to take it off.

MAUREEN. Major! *(He points to the other clothes.)* What?

MAJOR. Why don't you go into the office and get our receptionist?

MAUREEN. Oh, right.

*(She grabs the clothes on the hanger and rushes into the office.)*

MAJOR. She'll be out in a second.

SAM. *(Who has been listening in amazement to the last part of this conversation.)* You must be Mr. Cody.

MAJOR. Oh goodness me no old chap. I'm Ponsenby. Major Ponsenby of the 14th.

SAM. *(Pause.)* 14th what?

MAJOR. Her Majesty's 14th regiment of foot.

SAM. *(Pause.)* Foot?

MAJOR. Yes old chap, The P. B. I. You know.

SAM. *(Pause.)* P. B. I.?

MAJOR. Poor bloody infantry. The fighting 14th.

SAM. Right. Well, I'm Sam Lewis and this is Ashley, er — Mrs. Lewis.

MAJOR. A vision of loveliness. *(He takes her hand and kisses it.)* Enchanté Madame.

ASHLEY. *(Giggling.)* Oh, Sam. I do think we're going to like this place.

MAJOR. *(Looking at the card.)* I see you're from New York.

ASHLEY. That's right.

MAJOR. I loved a girl in New York once. *(Thoughtful.)* Well maybe twice. You remind me of her a little bit.

ASHLEY. Do I really?

MAJOR. We were engaged to be married. Very sad. Very sad.

ASHLEY. *(Pause.)* What was very sad?

MAJOR. She died the day after the wedding.

ASHLEY. Oh you poor man, you must have been devastated.

MAJOR. What?

ASHLEY. Well, to lose your wife after being married one day.

MAJOR. Not my wife old girl. We'd broken up a year before that. She married old Fotheringay. Very sad. Very sad.

ASHLEY. Oh, I see. I'm sorry.

MAJOR. You do remind me of her, though perhaps you are a little more beautiful.

SAM. Ahem! Is Mr. Cody here?

MAJOR. *(Looking over his shoulder he sees BRIAN beginning to stir.)* He's out at the moment. He's had a nasty shock recently, but I think he'll be coming around soon.

SAM. Good. Good.

*(Enter MAUREEN from the office. She is now in her "receptionist" outfit. A tailored blazer-type jacket with matching skirt and plain white blouse. She has one of the 3 x 5 cards in her hand.)*

MAJOR. Ah Maureen. This is Mr. Lewis. Here is his card.

*(Hands her the card.)*

MAUREEN. *(Takes the card.)* There's nothing written on it.

MAJOR. No — No. Here. *(He turns the card over.)*
MAUREEN. Why would they put the printing on the back of it?
MAJOR. Ahem. Why don't you check Mr. Lewis in, while I go and see if I can find Mr. Cody.

*(The MAJOR goes up the hall and tries to arouse BRIAN. There is little response, so he opens the door to room 8, drags BRIAN off the ladder, pushes him inside room 8, closes the door and exits U. L. carrying the ladder.)*

MAUREEN. *(Who has been standing smiling at SAM and ASH-LEY, suddenly remembers her cards. Reading:)* Good morning sir or madam. Welcome to the Turtle Beach Hotel. I am your receptionist. I am here to be of service. Would you kindly complete this form? *(She looks up and smiles.)*
SAM. *(Eventually.)* Yes, O.K. *(MAUREEN, frozen in place, continues to smile.)* The form?
ASHLEY. *(Moves behind the counter.)* I think she might be a bit new Sam. Let's see if I can help. Here we are.

*(She produces a form from the beneath the counter which SAM starts to complete.)*

MAUREEN. Thank you. You see, I've never done this before.
ASHLEY. There's nothing to it. Now, do you know which room we're in?
MAUREEN. You're in the reception area.
ASHLEY. No — no. Which room are we going to sleep in?
MAUREEN. I know. I know. Mrs. Cody told me.
ASHLEY. Yes?
MAUREEN. *(Very proud.)* You're in number 7. First on the right.
ASHLEY. Good. *(She takes a key from the board.)* All set Sam?
SAM. *(Puts down the pen.)* Right.

*(MAUREEN exits to the office. SAM and ASHLEY pick up their suit-cases and enter room 7. SAM puts his down U. S. of the dressing room door and closes the door to room 7. ASHLEY puts hers*

*down on the bed.)*

ASHLEY. What a lovely room.

SAM. Not bad. Not bad at all.

ASHLEY. *(Opens the dressing room door and switches on the light.)* Oh look Sam, a dressing room. A vanity and everything.

SAM. *(Unimpressed.)* Wonderful. *(He takes off his jacket and tie and leaves them on the bed, then wanders down to the French windows and looks out into the garden.)* Now that is nice. A little private patio, and you can see the beach.

ASHLEY. *(Now in the bathroom.)* The bathroom is so cute. Look Sam, its got pink wallpaper.

SAM. *(Gazing out of the French windows.)* Not bad, not bad at all.

ASHLEY. *(Comes just R. of him by the open window and puts her arm around him.)* Are you really going to buy this place?

SAM. Maybe pussycat, maybe. *(He turns and gives her a little peck on the cheek.)* Why don't you unpack and freshen up a little. I can't wait to explore the place.

ASHLEY. Alright. Don't be too long.

SAM. O.K. See you in a little bit. *(Gives her another quick kiss.)* I'll be down on the beach.

*(SAM exits out French windows. ASHLEY takes her suitcase off the bed, goes into the dressing room, returns for SAM'S jacket and tie, picks up SAM'S suitcase and exits to the dressing room, closing the door. Enter from the front entrance ABDUL EL HAJJ. It is, of course the MAJOR, now in Arab costume, a long flowing robe and a red and white chequered burnoose held by black bands. He carries a small suitcase. He rings the reception bell. MAUREEN enters from the office still in her receptionist outfit.)*

MAUREEN. Oh! It's just like that movie. The dark handsome Sheik comes to the rescue of the fair damsel in distress and carries her off to his harem in the desert.

ABDUL. My name is Abdul El Hajj. I would like a room please.

MAUREEN. *(Produces her card and reads:)* Good morning sir or madam. Welcome to the Turtle Beach Hotel. I am your receptionist. I am here to be service. Would you kindly complete this form?

ABDUL. Certainly.

MAUREEN. *(Just stands there for the longest time then — )* Oh, I know. Here. *(She produces a form and ABDUL starts to fill it in.)* You know you look just like the Major.

ABDUL. Really?

MAUREEN. Of course, you're much more handsome.

ABDUL. Thank you.

MAUREEN. *(Goes to look at the booking chart and comes back with a key which she hands to ABDUL.)* Here you are sir. You'll be in Room 6.

*(ASHLEY has come out of the dressing room. She picks up the bed-side phone and dials. It rings on the reception counter. MAUREEN picks it up.)*

MAUREEN. Turtle Beach Hotel.

ASHLEY. May I have room service please?

MAUREEN. Room service? Oh yes that's me. *(Looks at her clothes.)* Well, it will be in a minute,

ASHLEY. May I have some ice in room 7 please?

MAUREEN. Ice? Yes ma'am. Room seven. Yes· ma'am, right away ma'am.

*(She hangs up the phone and has the jacket off before she hurtles out of the office door. ABDUL continues to write. ASHLEY returns to the dressing room, leaving the door open. BRIAN emerges from room 8, comes R. and takes one look.)*

BRIAN. Major? Is that you? What the hell are you doing?

ABDUL. I beg your pardon.

BRIAN. Oh Major, I haven't got time for this. Mr. Lewis'll be here any moment and the Barracuda, and don't forget when she gets here, you've got a job to do. Now go and get changed will you.

ABDUL. I beg your pardon, sir!

BRIAN. You've had your little joke, but we've got things to do, remember Major?

ABDUL. I'm afraid I haven't the faintest idea what you're talking about.

BRIAN. *(Pauses briefly and has his first doubt.)* You know you do that very well, but we all agreed your job was to head the Barracuda off at the pass.

ABDUL. Are we speaking the same language sir?

BRIAN. Very funny Major.

ABDUL. As I have no intention of being funny, perhaps it would be better if we re-started this conversation from the beginning. Allow me to introduce myself. I am Abdul El Hajj, at your service.

*(He offers his hand with a slight bow.)*

BRIAN. *(Shakes hands.)* How do you do! I'm Brian Cody.

ABDUL. Ah, Mr. Cody. How pleased I am to meet you. I understand your charming little hotel is for sale. I want you to know that I am seriously interested in it, and a little later when I have completed my observations, I should like to talk business with you.

BRIAN. *(Really doubtful now and peering at ABDUL 'S face.)* Is it you or isn't it?

ABDUL. You're not making sense again Mr. Cody.

BRIAN. Well you've got me convinced Major. But Terri said not to do it, and every time we don't do as she says, you know we get into trouble, so why don't you just concentrate on the Barracuda.

ABDUL. I fail to see what diverting our attention to a fish has to do with our conversation.

BRIAN. What?

ABDUL. Are you confused sir?

BRIAN. Oh, I'm always confused. I say, you are the Major aren't you?

ABDUL. That's the third time you've asked me that question. I don't want to spend the rest of my life answering it. Please try to understand before one of us dies.

BRIAN. *(Looks at him.)* I think Terri had better handle this.

*(He turns to go into the office as MAUREEN, now in her room service outfit, hurtles out of the door and flattens him against the wall.*

*BRIAN holds his head and staggers into the office. ABDUL looks on in amazement and continues to complete his form. MAUREEN runs to the door of room 7 and knocks.)*

ASHLEY. Come in.

MAUREEN. *(Opens the door, steps in, takes out a card.)* Good morning sir or madam, I am your room service waitress, would you like to see the menu?

ASHLEY. *(Laughing.)* Are you new as well?

MAUREEN. Er — yes!

ASHLEY. I just wanted some ice.

MAUREEN. The ice! I forgot. *(She sprints back to the office. ABDUL picks up his key and exits to room 6 as MAUREEN re-appears with an ice bucket and sprints back to room 7.)* Here you are.

ASHLEY. Thank you.

MAUREEN. You're welcome. Would you like anything else?

ASHLEY. No thank you.

MAUREEN. Would Mr. Lewis like anything?

ASHLEY. No thank you. He's gone for a walk.

MAUREEN. O.K.

*(She just stands there.)*

ASHLEY. What is it?

MAUREEN. Well, I was wondering, if you needed anything later, from room service that is, maybe I could get it for you now.

ASHLEY. Why?

MAUREEN. It would save an awful lot of time.

ASHLEY. I'm sure it would, but if I need anything later, I'll call room service later.

MAUREEN. Yes ma'am.

*(MAUREEN leaves for the reception area. ASHLEY closes the door of room 7 and takes the ice with her into the bathroom, leaving the door open.)*

BRIAN. *(Coming out of the office.)* Where the hell were you going in such a hurry?

MAUREEN. *(Very proud.)* I'm room service sir.

BRIAN. Maybe you should just slow down the service a little. What on earth did the Major want at this time of day?

MAUREEN. Oh, it wasn't the Major sir. It was Mrs. Lewis.

BRIAN. Who?

MAUREEN. Mrs. Lewis.

BRIAN. They're here already?

MAUREEN. Yes, sir, in room seven.

BRIAN. *(Starting to panic again.)* Why didn't somebody tell me? I was supposed to meet him. *(Moving L.)* I'd better go and introduce myself. He'll expect to see me.

MAUREEN. He's not there sir.

BRIAN. *(Turning back.)* But you said —

MAUREEN. Mrs. Lewis is in room 7. Mr. Lewis has gone for a walk.

BRIAN. He's outside?

MAUREEN. Yes sir.

BRIAN. Damn. He'll probably fall down the hole. I'd better go and find him. You stay in charge here.

MAUREEN. I'm the receptionist again?

BRIAN. Yes.

*(MAUREEN dives for the office and exits. Enter the MAJOR from the front entrance.)*

MAJOR. Ah, Cody old chap. I was looking for you.

BRIAN. *(Looking him up down.)* That's much better Major. Now — no more of that Arab nonsense, eh?

MAJOR. Hang on old chap. What's all this about?

BRIAN. Never mind. I've got to find Mr. Lewis.

MAJOR. That's what I wanted to tell you. He's wandering about the garden.

BRIAN. *(Starting to panic and run around again.)* He's not supposed to be doing that. Heaven only knows what he'll find. I'm supposed to meet him first. I knew this was going to happen. Terri will be furious and —

MAJOR. Steady on old chap. Calm down. He seems like a nice old boy and his wife is an absolute crackerjack.

BRIAN. Something will go wrong. I just know it. Where was he?

MAJOR. Just out front.

BRIAN. I knew it. I knew it. That damn dog next door. He'll find it.

*(BRIAN EXITS out the front entrance on the dead run. TERRI enters from upstairs. She is now wearing an off-white linen suit, a turquoise silk blouse, hose, heels, an enormous wide-brimmed hat, and is absolutely dripping with jewelry.)*

TERRI. Hello Major. Where's Maureen? More to the point, where's Brian?

MAJOR. I say old girl, you look absolutely spiffing.

TERRI. *(Now downstairs and fussing behind the counter.)* Thank you. Where's Brian?

MAJOR. He's making a forward foray for the purposes of reconnaissance.

TERRI. For heaven's sake, Major, can't you speak English?

MAJOR. I might remind you madam that if anyone here can't speak English, it's certainly not me!

TERRI. I'm sorry. What I meant was, I didn't understand you.

MAJOR. Mr. Cody is outside looking for Mr. Lewis.

TERRI. Mr. Lewis? He's here already?

*(MAUREEN bursts out of the office, now back in her receptionist outfit, but has forgotten or not had time to put on the skirt. She is seen to be wearing a black lace teddy with garter belt and stockings. She dashes out from behind the counter in view of the audience.)*

TERRI. Maureen!

MAUREEN. *(Stops and turns.)* Yes ma'am?

*(TERRI just looks at her. MAUREEN eventually looks down, shrieks and rushes back into the office.)*

MAJOR. I say old girl. This the new uniform? Jolly good show, what? Reminds me of the time the Colonel's wife lost her drawers. Never saw anything like it, there she was standing in the middle of the polo field and this damned great dog jumped right up her skirt —

TERRI. Really Major. You must tell me about it sometime, but right now I'm more concerned with Mr. Lewis.

MAJOR. Ah, quite right old girl, but Mr. Cody has things in hand. He's gone to look for him so you don't have to worry.

TERRI. If Mr. Cody's gone to look for him, that's precisely why I do have to worry. *(MAUREEN enters from the office, now in the skirt and TERRI brings her out beyond the counter.)* Yes, that outfit looks very nice. Now, you're going to have to work in the dinning room this evening, so I'll have to find you something else to wear. I'll see if I can find something suitable and bring it down for you.

*(Enter SAM and BRIAN from the front entrance. TERRI moves L. so as to be well clear of the counter and steers MAUREEN behind it.)*

BRIAN. Yes sir, it's a little gold mine. It's just a pity that you won't be able to meet *(Sees TERRI.)* my wife! *(TERRI signals.)* She's — er — shopping in Miami. Yes sir, you know what they say, behind every successful man is a woman—with nothing to wear.

SAM. *(After an awkward pause.)* Aren't you going to introduce us?

BRIAN. Right. This is the Major. You've met him of course and this is er — er —

TERRI. *(Stepping forward towards SAM.)* I'm Mrs. Winthrop-Smythe. *(She pauses for effect.)* I'm from Palm Beach.

BRIAN. I would never have guessed.

SAM. *(Takes her hand.)* I'm delighted to meet you. *(Turns to BRIAN.)* You seem to have a very high class clientele Cody. You certainly seem to know how to run the place.

BRIAN. Oh I wouldn't say that.

TERRI. You say that all the time.

MAJOR. Right then. I'll be off now. Maureen, could you bring my afternoon tea to my room please?

*(Exit MAJOR U. L.)*

MAUREEN. *(Looks at BRIAN.)* Room service?

*(He nods and she hurtles into the office. HOPKINS enters down the stairs. He is totally transformed. He wears a dark suit, black shirt and a clerical collar, and carries a large Bible.)*

TERRI. Mr. Lewis. May I introduce you to the Reverend Hopkins.

SAM. How do you do Reverend? Are you staying in the hotel or do you live in town?

TERRI. The Reverend is a guest in the hotel, aren't you Reverend?

HOPKINS. *(In his best voice — attempting to sound "posh.")* Indeed I am. Indeed I am. You see the work I do is very hard. I'm rushed off my feet day and night, never get a minute to myself, and of course the rewards — oh, the rewards are meager you know, very meager. *(Looking at TERRI.)* and the worst part of my job is fixing broken bowls —

BRIAN. He means souls. He fixes broken souls.

TERRI. Cool it your eminence.

SAM. What?

BRIAN. She said he's a fool for penitence.

SAM. Oh. Well Cody, it's very refreshing to find that a man of the cloth should choose your place for his vacation. You could hardly have a better recommendation.

TERRI. Yes, that's what I thought.

SAM. Tell me Reverend, how do you spend your time here?

HOPKINS. I keep pretty busy, for instance, somewhere there always seems to be a leak in the john.

SAM. What?

BRIAN. He said he always reads St. Luke and St. John.

*(Enter ABDUL from room 6.)*

BRIAN. Oh no!

ABDUL. *(Strides right up to SAM and bows.)* Allow me to introduce myself. I am Abdul El Hajj. I am here for the buying of the hotel.

SAM. What?

TERRI. Brian, what's going on?

BRIAN. *(Grabs SAM and gently leads him U. L.)* Mr. Lewis you must be tired after your walk, why don't you go and freshen up a little? We can meet later and talk some business.

SAM. Good idea Cody.

BRIAN. *(Steering him to the door of room 7.)* It's a pity my wife can't be here to entertain Mrs. Lewis, but we really weren't expecting you today, and you know how these women are about their shopping.

SAM. *(Goes in room 7.)* No problem Cody. *(Closes the door and comes down to the open bathroom door.)* I'll be on the patio for a while.

*(Closes the door then exits French windows. BRIAN comes back R. from the door of room 7 and puts his arm around ABDUL'S shoulders.)*

BRIAN. Why don't you go back to your room. I'll send tea in as soon as it's ready.

ABDUL. Tea would be excellent, thank you.

*(Exit ABDUL to room 6. BRIAN comes R. to the counter and no one pays any attention to which room ABDUL goes in.)*

TERRI. Brian, I expect you to control the Major.

BRIAN. That's easier said than done my love. He keeps appearing out of nowhere, dressed in that ridiculous costume. How am I supposed to stop him?

HOPKINS. Maybe I should take him downtown with me.

TERRI. What good would that do?

HOPKINS. I thought it would keep him out of the way, you know, we could have a drink or something.

TERRI. The last thing we need is you and the Major drinking. Anyway, we need you here, and the Major is still our best bet to keep the Barracuda away from Mr. Lewis.

HOPKINS. I wouldn't mind volunteering for that job.

TERRI. No, Hopkins. We need you as the Reverend. Didn't you hear what Mr. Lewis said? He was impressed.

HOPKINS. Well, I'm not impressed. All I do is get to talk about sin, the Major actually gets to do it.

BRIAN. Oh come on, Hopkins. We're all in this together.

TERRI. *(Takes two keys from the rack.)* Here Hopkins, you take room 8. I'll take 11. Brian will you please get Maureen back in here.

*(Exit TERRI U.L. BRIAN exits to the office. HOPKINS looks carefully around, opens his Bible and takes out a bottle of liquor, has a good swallow, replaces it and exits to room 8 as MAUREEN, now in her room service outfit and carrying a tea tray, tears out of the office and exits U.L. Almost immediately the MAJOR enters from U.L. as HAYLEY enters from the front entrance. Age perhaps 35 — 45, she is attractive and smartly dressed. Sensuous and sexy, she is full-figured but not in any way cheap, tawdry or flashy. She wears a low-cut summer dress with a small bolero jacket and high heels. She carries a small fashionable suitcase.)*

HAYLEY. *(Drops her case by the counter near the front entrance.)* Major Ponsenby!

MAJOR. Miss Harrington!

HAYLEY. *(Advancing on him.)* I remember you.

MAJOR. *(Backing away.)* And I remember you.

HAYLEY. *(Stops and looks at him.)* Aren't you pleased to see little old Hayley back again?

MAJOR. Yes — yes. Of course.

HAYLEY. *(Advancing again.)* I won't bite you know. How about you and I getting together later?

MAJOR. Well — er — I'm rather tied up tonight.

HAYLEY. Oh goody. A bondage party!

MAJOR. Oh my God —

HAYLEY. I'm just teasing.

MAJOR. *(Circling to keep the chairs between them.)* Quite right old girl. Did I ever tell you about the time I was in Sidi-Berani —

*(HAYLEY has now reached him. She flings her arms around his neck and gives him a passionate kiss, full on the lips, as he falls backwards over one of the chairs. His head goes down, his legs go up*

*in the air as she falls over him, her legs between his. BRIAN comes out of the office, sees them, comes down and peers at them for the longest time as the MAJOR waves his arms and legs. BRIAN looks at the audience, shrugs his shoulders, salutes and returns to the office. Eventually the MAJOR and HAYLEY disentangle and stand up.)*

HAYLEY. Oh Major! It's just like old times. It really is nice to see you again. How about seeing me safely to my room?

MAJOR. You haven't got a room.

HAYLEY. *(Goes behind the counter and takes a key off the board.)* I do now.

MAJOR. But how do you know which one is yours?

HAYLEY. That's easy. I always have the same room every year. I book it a year in advance. I always stay in number seven.

MAJOR. Number seven?

HAYLEY. Yes, I call it my rumpus room!

MAJOR. Yes, but don't you think you ought to check with —

HAYLEY. Just give me a minute or two. Why don't you bring my bag? You big strong soldier boy.

*(She kisses him on the lips again, then goes to room 7, enters, closes the door and goes into the dressing room.)*

BRIAN. *(Peers round the office door, then enters.)* Ah Major. *(Comes out to the foot of the stairs.)* Been doing your duty I see.

MAJOR. Now look here Cody old chap. I'm not sure I can go through with this. I've known some women in my time, but this one is — er — er a bit much, if you know what I mean.

BRIAN. I know Major, but try to do your best. Remember your job is keeping her away from Mr. Lewis.

MAJOR. Yes, but who's job is it to keep her away from me?

BRIAN. Come off it Major! It can't be all that bad. You must admit, she's one hell of a good looking woman.

MAJOR. Damned attractive actually. Come to think of it old chap, you're right. I'd better learn to start enjoying my work.

MAUREEN. *(Enters from U.L. and comes R.)* Your tea is in your room Major.

MAJOR. Thank you my dear. I'll just have time for it. Looks like I'm going to have to keep my strength up.

*(Exit MAJOR U.L.)*

BRIAN. Right Maureen. You hold the fort here. I'm going to find Mrs. Cody.

MAUREEN. Reception?

BRIAN. Yes.

MAUREEN. Oh no!

*(She rushes into the office. BRIAN turns to go upstairs as HAYLEY comes out of the dressing room with a bundle of clothes on hangers over her arm and SAM'S suitcase in her other hand. She comes out of room 7, closes the door and comes down to the reception area.)*

HAYLEY. Mr. Cody, how nice to see you again.

BRIAN. *(Hurriedly getting back behind the counter.)* Miss Harrington. Welcome back. What can I do for you? *(HAYLEY stops dead in her tracks, looks at BRIAN, raises her eyebrows to the audience.)* Don't answer that. I mean, how can I be of service? *(HAYLEY looks at the audience again.)* I mean, what do you want?

HAYLEY. In answer to your three questions: One, I can think of lots of things you can do for me. Two, how you can be of service is an interesting question, but I'll leave that to you, and three, you should know by now what I want!

BRIAN. Oh my God!

HAYLEY. Oh relax. I'm just kidding. I don't think you're on my list this year. *(She drapes the clothes across the counter and drops the suitcase behind it.)* However, someone left a bunch of clothes in my room. Really Brian, you're slipping. You really will have to talk to the maid.

BRIAN. *(Confused.)* What? O.K. I'll do that. I'll find Mrs. Cody right away, she always deals with the staff.

*(He shuffles sideways to get past HAYLEY and escape up the stairs.*

*HAYLEY gives his rear a pinch as he goes by. Enter HOPKINS from room 8 still carrying his Bible. HAYLEY sees him coming and playfully ducks behind the counter. HOPKINS is now slightly tipsy and holds his liquor bottle, now empty, upside down. He comes D.R. to the reception area, wobbles just a little, then reaches down behind one of the chair cushions, finds a full bottle, puts the empty one back in its place, puts the new one carefully in his Bible and turns to see HAYLEY smiling at him.)*

HAYLEY. Well, well. A clergyman. Are you a Reverend?

HOPKINS. Oh yes. Very reverend.

HAYLEY. This is one of my fantasies.

HOPKINS. Really?

HAYLEY *(Looks him up and down and then has a terrible thought.)* You're not Catholic are you?

HOPKINS. I'm Episcapoleon, I mean Apascapilion, I mean Opiscapoolian. *(He pauses.)* I'm reformed.

HAYLEY. *(Advancing on him.)* Well I'm not! *(Runs her finger round his collar.)* How would you like to hold services with me a little later?

HOPKINS. Me?

HAYLEY. You know I've always had this thing for clergyman.

HOPKINS. How nice. What thing?

HAYLEY. Come now Reverend. You know what I mean. You and I should definitely have an organ recital together.

HOPKINS. You're putting me on.

HAYLEY. That can be arranged too. Why don't we say my room. Number seven in about fifteen minutes?

HOPKINS. Right. Fifteen minutes. I think I'll just take a little walk outside to cool off. I seem to be a little hot under the collar.

*(Exit HOPKINS front entrance. Enter ABDUL from room 6. HAY-LEY'S eyes light up.)*

ABDUL. Good afternoon madam. May I introduce myself. I am Abdul El Hajj, The Lion of the Desert, at your service.

HAYLEY. *(Takes his proffered hand.)* You look just like —

ABDUL. And you madam, look just like the desert rose in the first blush of full bloom.

HAYLEY. Oh my! I'm Hayley.

ABDUL. Hayley — Hayley — Such a beautiful name. You know there's an Arabic word pronounced much the same as Hayley.

HAYLEY. Really. What does it mean?

ABDUL. Well, loosely translated —"The gentle parting of ruby red lips beneath the dark cloudless sky of the new moon."

HAYLEY. Oh my!

ABDUL. Would you permit me to accompany you on a stroll down to the beach?

HAYLEY. *(Looking at her watch.)* Well I had arranged to — oh what the hell — why not. But I have to be back in ten minutes.

*(They both exit front entrance arm in arm. MAUREEN comes out of the office in her receptionist outfit and sees the clothes on the counter. She picks up the dress, holds it up in front of her, smiles, picks up all the clothes and exits to the office as TERRI enters U.L. and BRIAN comes downstairs.)*

TERRI. Ah, there you are Brian. Have you talked with Mr. Lewis yet?

BRIAN. No, but I've arranged to meet him later.

TERRI. *(Busy with papers etc. behind the counter.)* I really think we've impressed him. Even Hopkins seemed to pull it off.

BRIAN. Talking of Hopkins, you might be right. I think he's been drinking again.

TERRI. Well, we've done everything we can. The bar's all locked up during the day, there's absolutely no way he can get his hands on any booze till he clocks out at six.

BRIAN. Oh well, I hope you're right.

TERRI. Has the Barracuda put a move on you yet?

BRIAN. No, she says I'm not on her list this year.

TERRI. Good. *(Comes over to him.)* Just make sure you're never on anyone's list but mine.

BRIAN. Oh Terri. *(He puts his hands on her shoulders and gazes into her eyes.)*

TERRI. You know, sometimes you can be very maddening, but I do love you, you idiot.

*(They kiss and hold it. Enter SAM from the patio, he opens the bathroom door.)*

SAM. I'm going to talk to Cody. Why don't you put on that new outfit and I'll be back with a couple of drinks.

ASHLEY. *(Appears in the bathroom doorway wearing only a towel.)* Oh, Sam, I really do like this place. Do you think you might buy it?

SAM. Maybe pussycat, maybe.

ASHLEY. *(Strikes a seductive pose against the door frame.)* Why don't we — you know, take a nap?

SAM. Ah, well, perhaps a bit later dear.

ASHLEY. *(Sighs.)* Well if you change your mind you know where I am.

*(She blows him a kiss and returns to the bathroom.)*

SAM. Er — right. Bye. *(He exits room 7, closes the door and comes R. to the reception area. He sees BRIAN and TERRI.)* Excuse me. *(They break apart.)* Well, well, well, Mrs. Winthrop-Smythe and Mr. Cody! The wife is shopping in Miami and you're shopping in the Keys? And you Mrs. Winthrop-Smythe, I've heard about what goes on in Palm Beach, but now I get to see it with my own eyes.

BRIAN. Now really Mr. Lewis. I can explain.

TERRI. No Mr. Cody, let me. Mr. Lewis, Mr. Cody is totally innocent. I am entirely to blame. The romantic atmosphere of this charming little inn simply got the better of me.

SAM. My dear Mrs. Winthrop-Smythe. We really must learn to control our animal impulses. *(ASHLEY has come out of the bathroom and entered the dressing room.)* Though I must say that my wife too seems to be affected by this place.

*(ASHLEY has come out of the dressing room, opened the door of room 7 and is standing there in the doorway.)*

ASHLEY. Sam! Sam!
SAM. Excuse me. *(He hurries to room 7.)* What is it?
ASHLEY. My clothes. They're gone.
SAM. What?
ASHLEY. Gone.

*(SAM quickly looks in the dressing room, then returns to the reception area as ASHLEY sits dejectedly on the bed.)*

SAM. Mr. Cody, has the maid been in our room?
BRIAN. I don't know. Why?
SAM. My wife's clothes are gone.
BRIAN. Oh dear. *(Calling to the office door.)* Maureen, could you come here for a moment please.
MAUREEN. *(Puts her head round the door.)* Maid, reception or room service?
BRIAN. Right now it doesn't matter. *(MAUREEN enters in her receptionist outfit.)* Have you been in room seven?
MAUREEN. Yes sir.
BRIAN. When?
MAUREEN. I took some ice in to Mrs. Lewis.
BRIAN. No. No after that?
MAUREEN. No sir.
BRIAN. Oh dear. This is most upsetting.
TERRI. I'm sure there's some perfectly innocent explanation.

BRIAN. *(Starting to panic.)* What are we going to do? Everything's starting to fall apart. We can't have clothes disappearing all over the place, what —

TERRI. You know Mr. Cody. I was once is a very similar situation —

BRIAN. You never told me —

TERRI. In a hotel in Palm Springs. The management temporarily mislaid my bags and do you know what they did?

BRIAN. *(Pause.)* No, but I've got a very strong feeling you're going to tell us.

TERRI. They sent a complimentary bottle of champagne to my room while they found them.

BRIAN. Really? *(Pause. TERRI is "winding him" on with her hands.)* Oh — yes — right. Mr. Lewis, why don't you wait in your room. I'll have a complimentary bottle of champagne sent in right away, while we find your wife's clothes.

SAM. Excellent. Excellent. You certainly know how to treat your guests Cody.

BRIAN. If you don't want to sit in your room you can have it on your patio, it's very private.

SAM. Excellent. *(Claps BRIAN on the shoulders.)* Fine hotel you've got here Cody.

*(He goes U.L., enters room 7, takes ASHLEY by the hand and they exit through the French windows.)*

MAUREEN. I suppose you want me to take the champagne to room 7? *(BRIAN nods.)* Room service?

*(BRIAN and TERRI both nod.)*

TERRI. While you change, get out two bottles please. We'll have one as well. *(MAUREEN exits to the office.)* I think we deserve something, don't you darling?

*(They sit in the two chairs, TERRI L. and BRIAN R.)*

BRIAN. What were you doing in Palm Springs?

TERRI. I've never been to Palm Springs.

BRIAN. You mean you just made up that story about the champagne?

TERRI. *(Laughs.)* I was just trying to help you darling.

BRIAN. I must say you were pretty quick.

TERRI. I think we're going to pull it off. Mr. Lewis really seems to like the place. By the way, has he met the Barracuda yet?

BRIAN. I don't think so. The Major seems to be doing a pretty good job.

TERRI. Talking about the Major, we've got to stop him from getting dressed up in that ridiculous Arab outfit. If we're not careful, he's liable to give everything aw. ,.

BRIAN. Are you sure it is the Major?

TERRI. Of course it's the Major. Who else could it be?

BRIAN. You don't think it could be his twin brother do you?

TERRI. Really Brian. You don't believe that incredible story. And anyway, have you ever seen them together?

BRIAN. Come to think of it. No. I guess you're right, it's just that he acts as if he doesn't know me.

TERRI. He's just playing out his little fantasy. But it's dangerous. If we can see through it so easily, Mr. Lewis probably can too.

BRIAN. Well, his motives are good. He did say he wanted to drive the price up.

TERRI. The only thing he's liable to drive up is me, — up the wall.

*(MAUREEN, looking a little frazzled, comes out of the office in her room service outfit. She dumps two trays on the counter. They contain two open bottles of champagne in ice buckets and at least seven glasses.)*

BRIAN. *(Gets up to help her.)* Here, let help you with that. Here you go, number seven. They're probably on the patio.

*(During the following conversation MAUREEN takes one tray, one bottle in its ice bucket and two glasses into room 7, out onto the patio, then back in, out of room 7 closing the door and finally exits to the office.)*

TERRI. Come on Brian. Let's relax for a few minutes.

BRIAN. *(Goes up to the counter to pour the champagne.)* O.K.

TERRI. And then we've got to do something about those clothes.

BRIAN. Yeah. That's a funny thing isn't it.

TERRI. What do you think of him?

BRIAN. Who? Mr. Lewis?

TERRI. Yes.

BRIAN. Oh, I dunno. Bit straight-laced isn't he? "We must control our animal impulses."

TERRI. Well, he's just about our last hope to sell this place, so let's go along with him and try to keep him happy.

*(BRIAN has poured the champagne and is standing with a glass in each hand just prior to handing TERRI hers. The MAJOR enters from the front entrance. BRIAN half turns toward him.)*

MAJOR. *(Takes the glass in BRIAN'S right hand.)* Thanks old chap.

*(And without a breaking stride continues on and exits U.L. BRIAN shrugs, pours another glass and is standing again with a glass in each hand as HOPKINS enters from the front entrance. BRIAN turns.)*

HOPKINS. *(Takes the glass in BRIAN'S right hand.)* Very sociable of you Mr. C.

*(And without breaking stride continues on and exits to room 8. BRIAN pours another glass and once again has a glass in each hand as HAYLEY enters from the front entrance. BRIAN turns. HAYLEY picks up her suitcase with her left hand then takes the glass in BRIAN'S right hand with her right hand.)*

HAYLEY. Thanks. They say you shouldn't go to work on an empty stomach.

*(And without breaking stride continues on to room 7, exits into the bathroom and closes the door.)*

BRIAN. If you want some champagne, you'd better drink it straight from the bottle!

*(He hands her his glass and pours himself another one. He sits and they both drink.)*

TERRI. I've been thinking. Mr. Lewis having some champagne is probably a better idea then we thought. It'll put him in a good mood for your negotiations.

BRIAN. I wish you could be there.

TERRI. Well I can't. Not so long as I'm Mrs. Winthrop-Smythe.

BRIAN. Where did you get that name?

TERRI. Oh, I don't know. Isn't every woman in Palm Beach Mrs. Winthrop-something?

BRIAN. I don't know. I don't think I've ever met anyone from Palm Beach. Aren't they all supposed to be in bed with someone else's husband?

TERRI. *(Laughs.)* Well then we created the right impression for the very prim and proper Mr. Lewis.

BRIAN. Yes, but imagine what's going to happen if the Barracuda gets her hands on the very prim and proper Mr. Lewis.

TERRI. Well, so far, the Major seems to be doing the job. *(She stands.)* You know, I've just had a thought. The only place I can think of for those clothes is the laundry room. I'll go and look.

*(She exits U. L. BRIAN sips his champagne. Enter ABDUL from the front entrance.)*

BRIAN. Ah, there you are. Are you happy in your work? Keeping the Barracuda busy?

ABDUL. *(Stares at him for a moment.)* Mr. Cody, have you noticed that you and I seem to keep having these dialogues in which only you participate? I might remind you that the word dialogue is prefaced by the letters d and i — di, from the Greek meaning two, and logos from the Greek meaning words. Much as I would like to join you in conversation, I never seem to have the faintest idea what you're talking about.

BRIAN. *(Stands and goes up very close to him.)* How about that. You aren't the Major are you?

ABDUL. There, you see, that's what I mean.

BRIAN. And you're not doing this just to drive the price up?

ABDUL. Mr. Cody. I think you must be living in the ozone layer. Either that or you've been drinking too much of that champagne.

BRIAN. The resemblance is quite amazing.

ABDUL. Mr. Cody. I like your little hotel very much. I think perhaps it has great potential, and I was definitely considering making you a very serious offer, but how we are to communicate with each other, I just don't know.

*(Exit ABDUL to room 6. BRIAN exits to the office. TERRI enters from U.L. knocks on the door of room 7 and opens the door.)*

TERRI. Mrs. Lewis? *(She comes down as ASHLEY, still wearing a towel, comes in from the patio followed by SAM.)* Oh, Mrs. Lewis. Mr. Cody seems unable to find your clothes for the moment, and he asked me to take you up to Mrs. Cody's room and help you find something to wear.

ASHLEY. Thank you. That's very kind.

SAM. Take your time dear. All the fresh air, and then the champagne has made me feel quite sleepy. I think I'm going to take a little nap.

*(TERRI and ASHLEY exit room 7. SAM takes off his pants, shoes and socks, puts them in the dressing room, gets into bed in the center of the bed and pulls the covers right up.)*

TERRI. *(As they make their way upstairs.)* Mr. Cody tells me you're about the same size as Mrs. Cody, so we shouldn't have any problems.

ASHLEY. You know it's really quite funny. Here I am, walking around a hotel without a stitch on. I mean not a stitch! *(She giggles.)*

TERRI. Well, I'm just glad you've managed to keep your sense of humor.

*(They exit talking, upstairs. Enter from the French windows, the MAJOR. He tips-toes to the bed, sees the sleeping figure, and proceeds to strip down to his underwear. Singing softly to himself the overture from Carmen, he peels off, with a flourish, his shoes, socks, shirt and pants, mimicking the actions of a strip-tease dancer. His underwear is complete with arm patches, badges of rank and medal ribbons. He has a large Union Jack sewn right across the seat of his boxer shorts. He pulls the bed clothes back a little on the right side of the bed prior to getting in and sits facing right.*
*HOPKINS has come out of room 8 in his socks and underwear, but still wearing his clerical collar. He comes D.R. just a little, listens, then goes back to the door of room 7. The MAJOR gets into bed only a split second before HOPKINS opens the door and leaps into bed on the left side as:*
*HAYLEY comes out of the bathroom, wearing nothing but a robe.*

*She stands just R. of the bathroom door with her back to the audience as the three in bed sit up and yell. She flings open her robe and stands there as the three in bed react.*

HAYLEY. Don't start without me boys!

*(The curtain falls.)*

## ACT II

### Scene 1

*(While the action is continuous, the doorknob on the inside of room 7 has been loosened so as to come right off in HOPKINS hand on page 56. BRIAN, hearing the screams, comes running out of the office and flings open the door of room 7. He stops dead in his tracks and stares in disbelief at HAYLEY, who remains with her back to the audience and her robe held wide open.)*

· BRIAN. Oh my dear Lord—

*(He stands with both hands raised in front of him, with fingers outstretched, then realizes what a suggestive pose this is and, trying to be nonchalant, quickly puts his hands behind his back.)*

HAYLEY. Oh well! What's one more? *(She now nods to the bed where R. to L., the MAJOR has his hands almost on top of his head, the heels covering his ears and his mouth wide open, SAM has covered his eyes and HOPKINS has his hands over his mouth.)* What's this? Hear no evil, see no evil, speak no evil? *(She closes her robe and walks to the foot of the bed, R. corner.)* The Major and the Reverend I know, but I don't think we've been introduced.

SAM. I'm Sam Lewis. I'm pleased to meet you. *(He offers his hand.)*

HAYLEY. *(Reaches out to shake his hand and the robe falls open again. Sam shakes hands with his left hand over his eyes.)* Well, Mr. Sam Lewis, under normal circumstances, I'd be pleased to meet you, but judging by what I see going on here, I'm not so sure.

SAM. Well, judging by what I see, I'm definitely pleased to meet you.

HAYLEY. *(Closes her robe and nods to the other two.)* That's not quite what I meant.

SAM. *(Looking at the other two in the bed.)* You're not suggest-ing — that I — that we — that's outrageous!

MAJOR. Steady on old girl, we don't want you jumping to con-clusions you know.

HAYLEY. I'm absolutely delighted to hear that, now —

BRIAN. *(Starting in a very soft calm voice.)* Excuse me, do you think it might be possible, if it's not too much trouble, to interrupt this stroll down mammary lane, and if I wouldn't be inconveniencing any-body, for someone to tell me — *(Now yelling.)* what the hell is going on here? You know you guys are incredible, you're only after one thing.

HAYLEY. *(Facing U.L. opens her robe and looks down.)* What's wrong with the other one?

*(Enter down the stairs TERRI and ASHLEY. ASHLEY is still wearing her towel but carries some other clothes, a small bundle of what might be underwear and one dress on a hanger. As they reach the foot of the stairs, BRIAN, who is still in the open doorway of room 7, hears them coming and starts to panic.)*

BRIAN. Oh my God! They're coming, — quick — *(To HAY-LEY.)* For heaven's sake, cover yourself up. My wife will kill me.

SAM. So will mine.

*(BRIAN closes and locks the door. There is a general panic in the room. TERRI exits U.L. ASHLEY tries to open the door, finds it locked, then knocks.)*

ASHLEY. Sam, it's me. Let me in.

*(HAYLEY has gone into the bathroom and closed the door. BRIAN goes into the dressing room and closes the door. The MAJOR and HOPKINS lie down under the covers. SAM sits up in the middle of the bed. In their haste, two bare feet protrude out of the bottom of the bed next to each other. They are both left feet!)*

SAM. Come in.

ASHLEY. *(Rattles the door.)* It's locked.

SAM. Mr. Cody. *(BRIAN puts his head around the dressing room door.)* The door! *(BRIAN goes to the door, turns the key and quickly ducks back into the dressing room, closing the door.)* It's O.K. now dear.

ASHLEY. *(Comes in, leaves the door ajar and, barely glancing at the bed, heads straight for the bathroom.)* Well, I've got a dress to wear, won't be a minute.

SAM. No!

ASHLEY. *(Her hand on the bathroom doorknob, turns.)* What?

SAM. You — er — don't want to go in there.

ASHLEY. I need to get dressed Sam.

SAM. No you don't.

ASHLEY. What?

SAM. You don't need to get dressed.

ASHLEY. I don't?

SAM. No.

ASHLEY. Why not?

SAM. Well, er — *(Sexy:)* You know.

ASHLEY. *(Comes up to the bed.)* Well, well, Sam Lewis. I don't know what's gotten into you today. Feeling romantic? In the middle of the afternoon? There's life in the old boy yet, huh?

SAM. Well dear, you know how it is.

ASHLEY. *(Walks round to the R. side of the bed looking at the feet.)* Why do I get the feeling something is wrong?

SAM. There's nothing wrong dear.

ASHLEY. *(Still staring at the feet, comes round to the L. side of the bed.)* I can't quite put my finger on it. *(Turns.)* I'll be right back.

*(She heads toward the bathroom as SAM covers up the feet.)*

> SAM. You'll never miss her.
> ASHLEY. What did you say?
> SAM. I said you're a clever kisser! Kiss me my love.

*(He leans as far as he can over HOPKINS on the L. side of the bed and puckers up.)*

> ASHLEY. You really mean it don't you? *(She comes up to the L. side of the bed and kisses him, then drops the clothes on the bed. SAM snaps his finger behind her back and BRIAN puts his head out of the dressing room door.)* What was that?

*(She turns as BRIAN ducks out of sight. SAM takes advantage of her momentary distraction to climb over HOPKINS and get out of bed.)*

> SAM. Just my heart beating my love!

*(He embraces her with a long passionate kiss which starts with SAM R. and ASHLEY L. As BRIAN comes out of the dressing room and moves to the door of room 7, SAM keeps ASHLEY turned so her back is always toward BRIAN. SAM gives BRIAN hand signals to direct him to the door. BRIAN slowly opens the door, slides out and exits to the office as SAM kicks the door shut with his foot.)*

> ASHLEY. *(Breaks off and looks at the door.)* What was that?
> SAM. *(Slaps the door with his hand.)* Ants! Pesky little creatures.

*(He leaps up and down stamping madly.)*

ASHLEY. I can't see them.

SAM. Well — er — you had your eyes closed.

ASHLEY. Didn't you?

SAM. Yes, but I could hear them. *(Stamping again.)* That's about the last of them.

ASHLEY. *(Puts her arm around him.)* Never mind the ants. Let's see now, where were we?

SAM. *(Pulling away.)* Well — er — maybe later dear. *(Picks up the dress and hands it to her.)* Why don't you get dressed?

ASHLEY. What happened to the romantic mood? You just told me not to get dressed.

SAM. *(He opens the dressing room door.)* Yes, but — er — now — I think maybe you'd better.

ASHLEY. O.K. Talk about hot and cold!

*(She heads for the bathroom. SAM gets to her just as her hand is on the doorknob.)*

SAM. Not in there. *(ASHLEY frowns at him.)* What's the point of having a dressing room if we don't use it to put a dress on? *(ASHLEY pauses, her hand still on the doorknob, then goes into the dressing room. SAM follows her to make sure the door is closed then rushes to the bed and shakes it.)* Quick, everybody out. *(He rushes to the bathroom and opens the door.)* Hurry.

*(HOPKINS grunts and rolls over to the R. side of the bed.)*

MAJOR. *(Getting out of the bed R. side.)* I say old chap, close call what? *(Picks up his clothes.)*

HAYLEY. *(Comes out of the bathroom and strikes a pose in the doorway.)* This is fun. What are we going to do next big boy?

SAM. You're going to leave. *(Points to the dressing room door.)* That's my wife in there.

MAJOR. Dashed exciting old chap. Did I ever tell you about

thrill a minute Parkinson? He had this girl you see, they were standing up in a hammock at the time and —

SAM. I'm sure that's very interesting Major, but we are a little pressed for time. I have no idea why you're here, or what you're doing, but I want you to leave. Now!

MAJOR. Right old chap. *(Sighs.)* I suppose it's time to go to work. Would you care to join me in my room Miss Harrington. I'm in number 10.

HAYLEY. Major, you're my kind of guy. Give me a minute. I'll just get my things.

*(She goes into the bathroom, closing the door. The MAJOR waits for her outside the bathroom door.)*

SAM. *(Now back at the bed.)* Hey — you — good grief. He's asleep. Come on —

*(ASHLEY, still in her towel, opens the dressing room door. The MAJOR slips quickly out of the French windows. SAM, who is kneeling on the bed facing R., rolls HOPKINS off the bed onto the floor, then leans back on the pillows trying to look nonchalant. His right hand is over the edge of the bed motioning for HOPKINS to get under it, which he does.)*

ASHLEY. *(Getting into bed.)* Sam, I've been thinking. What's the hurry? I think I feel like taking a nap too. Besides there's something exciting about love in the afternoon.

*(They sit up in bed and kiss. SAM maneuvers ASHLEY so she doesn't see HAYLEY come out of the bathroom carrying her suitcase and exit through the French windows. HOPKINS emerges from under the L. side of the bed. SAM turns ASHLEY again. HOPKINS tiptoes to the door. The doorknob comes off in his hand. He stands there and shows it to SAM. SAM signals him to go out of the*

*French windows. He puts the doorknob on the table and goes down to the French windows. ASHLEY breaks off the kiss and almost sees him, but SAM grabs her again and turns her away. HOPKINS stops, looks down, realizes he is in his underwear, creeps back to the dressing room, reappears with ASHLEY'S dress, wraps it around his middle and exits through the French windows. As soon as SAM sees him leave, he breaks away from ASHLEY and gets out of bed.)*

ASHLEY. Now what?

SAM. I think I ought to get ready for my meeting with Mr. Cody.

ASHLEY. Sam Lewis. I do declare, I just can't figure you out today!

SAM. I know. Wait a minute my love. (*He rushes out of the French windows and returns immediately with the tray containing the champagne in the ice bucket and two glasses, which he places on the L. bedside table.*) Here you are my dear. We never finished it. Why don't you have some more?

*(He pours her a glass.)*

ASHLEY. Aren't you going to have some?

SAM. No, not for me thanks, not when I'm on the job.

ASHLEY. *(Giggles.)* Ooh, that's when I enjoy it the most!

SAM. Well, I've got work to do.

ASHLEY. Really Sam. You're in a strange mood today. You're up and down like a yo-yo.

SAM. *(Going into the dressing room.)* Yes well, — er – I'm just a bit excited dear.

ASHLEY. About buying this place? *(She sips her champagne.)* Oh, I do hope so. Here I am, in the middle of the afternoon, sitting in bed, drinking champagne. I could really get used to this you know.

SAM. *(In the doorway of the dressing room, putting on his shirt and pants.)* Well, it's still a bit early. I need to get more information about this place. I need to find out what's going on here. I think I'm going to try to talk to one or two of the guests as well as Cody.

ASHLEY. Have you met any of them yet?

SAM. *(Now sitting on the edge of the bed putting on his shoes and socks.)* Well, yes, a couple of them.

ASHLEY. What are they like?

SAM. Well. *(He pauses and reflects.)* Come to think of it, they're about the strangest bunch I've ever met.

ASHLEY. What do you mean?

SAM. Well, it's difficult to say really, but they all seem like sex maniacs.

ASHLEY. What? *(Laughing.)* The only one I've met is Mrs. Winthrop-What's It, and I really can't imagine her being a sex maniac.

SAM. *(Gets up and goes to the door, realizes the knob is missing then sees it on the table and hides it behind his back.)* You'd be surprised. They do it in Palm Beach you know, just like anywhere else in the world. Probably more because they've got more bedrooms. Anyway, I'm going to see who I can find to talk to. *(Gives her a little kiss.)* See you later.

*(Exit French windows. ASHLEY stays in bed sipping her champagne. Enter ABDUL from room 6. He comes down to the reception counter and rings the bell. MAUREEN comes out of the office. She is in her receptionist outfit.)*

ABDUL. Excuse me Miss, but some while ago Mr. Cody promised me that some tea would be sent to my room. Perhaps you could take care of it for me?

MAUREEN. *(Dreamily, once again enraptured by ABDUL.)* Oh yes sir. Anything at all sir. *(She looks at him.)*

ABDUL. Thank you.

MAUREEN. You know, if you don't mind me saying so, your

voice sounds just like the Major's.

ABDUL. Really?

MAUREEN. Yes, you look a bit like him too.

ABDUL. Perhaps you should tell me about this "Major". What is his name?

MAUREEN. I don't know. We all just call him "The Major." Do you have four wives?

ABDUL. I beg your pardon?

MAUREEN. Somebody told me you're allowed to have four wives.

ABDUL. Ah, I see. No, I don't have four wives. As a matter of fact, I don't have a wife at all.

MAUREEN. O-o-o-h. The tall dark handsome Sheik —

ABDUL. Please don't start that again. I can assure you I have no intention of carrying anyone off to my harem in the desert.

MAUREEN. You wouldn't have to carry me off. I'd come willingly.

ABDUL. *(Teasing.)* Ah, but would you love me when I got old?

MAUREEN. That depends on what it is you got hold of.

ABDUL. Yes well, the tea my dear?

MAUREEN. Yes sir.

*(As ABDUL turns to go, HAYLEY enters from the front entrance still in her robe and carrying her suitcase.)*

HAYLEY. *(Seeing ABDUL.)* Well hello again big boy!

ABDUL. Ah, The Desert Rose. Hello.

HAYLEY. *(Comes U. L. to him)* I'm sorry I had to rush off earlier. I — er — had a previous commitment.

ABDUL. No apology is necessary. Perhaps we can renew our acquaintance once I'm free of my business responsibilities.

HAYLEY. Oh, you have business in this hotel too?

ABDUL. Yes indeed. As a mater of fact, I'm looking into the possibility of buying it.

HAYLEY. Well, well. I could probably be of help to you. I've been coming here for years. I can tell you all about the place.

*(MAUREEN is shaking her head at ABDUL who does not notice.)*

ABDUL. Excellent, perhaps we should meet later and discuss a little business?

HAYLEY. I'm almost certain to be busy later. Are you free now?

*(MAUREEN is mouthing "no—no—no" to ABDUL.)*

ABDUL. Well, yes, but I thought — er — that is — are you really dressed for business?

HAYLEY. I'm most definitely dressed for business.

ABDUL. Then you must forgive me. I'm obviously not used to some of your western customs.

HAYLEY. You will be soon! Your room?

ABDUL. But of course.

*(He goes to room 6, opens the door and stands waiting for HAYLEY to enter. She pauses, winks at the audience, licks her lips, picks up her suitcase and enters, followed by ABDUL who closes the door.*

*ASHLEY gets off the bed, goes into the dressing room, gives a cry of desperation, comes out and goes to the door of room 7. She finds the doorknob missing and storms out of the French windows.*

*Enter HOPKINS from the front entrance dressed as before, clutching the dress about his waist, looking around hoping no one will see him. When he sees MAUREEN, he puts his finger to his lips, then goes past with a finger wave. He exits room 8.*

*Enter the MAJOR from the front entrance, still in his underwear and carrying his clothes and shoes. He motions to MAUREEN to keep quiet and creeps furtively off U.L.*

*Enter ASHLEY from the front entrance, still in her towel.)*

MAUREEN. Doesn't anybody wear clothes any more?

ASHLEY. It's gone again.

MAUREEN. What?

ASHLEY. It's gone again. My dress.

MAUREEN. Oh dear.

ASHLEY. I think perhaps, you'd better find Mr. Cody.

MAUREEN. Yes, of course. *(Opens the office door.)* Mr. Cody!

ASHLEY. I really don't understand it, it was there one minute and gone the next.

BRIAN. *(Enters from the office.)* Ah, Mrs. Lewis. What seems to be the towel? I mean trouble, what seems to be the trouble?

ASHLEY. I've lost my dress again.

MAUREEN. It's not lost.

ASHLEY. It most definitely is.

MAUREEN. What I mean is, I know where it is.

BRIAN. *(Pauses, waiting.)* Well?

MAUREEN. Hopkins is wearing it.

BRIAN. What?

MAUREEN. The not so reverend Hopkins.

BRIAN. *(Starting to panic again.)* Oh dear, this is terrible. Why can't anyone keep their clothes on today. We need Terri to sort this out. I mean — er — I'll go and get Mrs. Winthrop-Smythe. Maureen, why don't you take Mrs. Lewis upstairs to Mrs. Cody's room and get another dress.

*(MAUREEN and ASHLEY exit upstairs. BRIAN exits U.L. on the dead run. The door to room 6 opens and ABDUL, his clothes in disarray, his burnoose slightly off center, starts to slip out of the door. He is pulled back in by the unseen HAYLEY and the door closes as BRIAN and TERRI enter U. L. and come down to the reception area.)*

TERRI. Really Brian. How can she have lost another dress?

BRIAN. I don't know. I sent her upstairs again with Maureen. You know, there's a lot of strange things going on.

TERRI. Don't be silly. There's nothing going on.

BRIAN. That shows how much you know. Mrs. Lewis has been wearing a towel since the moment she got here. Maureen says Hopkins is wearing a dress. The Barracuda has taken up flashing. The Major is prancing around in his underwear, and you say nothing is going on. *(He collapses on her shoulder.)* I don't think I can take much more of this.

TERRI. *(Putting her arm around him.)* Of course you can. Things are actually going quite well. You're doing just fine.

*(She gives him a little kiss. Enter SAM from the front entrance.)*

SAM. It never stops in this place. Mr. Cody! Mrs. Winthrop-Smythe! At it again I see!

TERRI. *(Stares coldly at SAM.)* I'm going to help your wife select some more clothes. She appears to have lost her dress again.

*(Exit TERRI upstairs.)*

SAM. Really, Mr. Cody. I'm surprised at you.

BRIAN. It's all perfectly innocent.

SAM. Let's not go through that again. I have a problem.

*(He holds up the doorknob.)*

BRIAN. *(Pause.)* It's a doorknob.

*(MAUREEN comes downstairs.)*

SAM. Yes Mr. Cody. It's a doorknob.

BRIAN. I see. *(Pause. He takes the doorknob and looks at it.)* Well it's a nice doorknob. Don't you think it's a nice doorknob Maureen? Mind you, not that I'm a great expert on doorknobs, but if you're a collector, I suppose —

SAM. I don't mean it's my doorknob. I mean it's from the door of my room. Number seven.

BRIAN. I see. *(Pause.)* May I ask why you took it off?

SAM. I didn't take it off. It came off.

BRIAN. Oh, I see. Well, we'll just have to get it fixed. Maureen could you find Hopkins — er — our maintenance man please? *(MAUREEN exits U. L.)* Sorry about that.

SAM. That's alright. As a matter of fact, I'm glad you're here. Why don't we sit down for a few minutes and have that little chat we were talking about.

BRIAN. Right.

*(They sit in the two chairs. The door of room 6 opens and ABDUL staggers out. He is now in total disarray. His burnoose askew, he leans on the doorframe gasping for breath. HAYLEY pulls him back in and closes the door.)*

SAM. Now, let's get down to business. This is a very interesting little place you've got here Cody, but there are one or two questions I'd like to ask you.

BRIAN. Oh dear!

SAM. Yes, for instance —

*(He is interrupted by MAUREEN who comes running down form U.L.)*

MAUREEN. Oh Mr. Cody.

BRIAN. What is it Maureen?

MAUREEN. *(Looking at SAM.)* Well — er — er —

BRIAN. Did you find our maintenance man?

MAUREEN. Oh yes, I found him alright.

BRIAN. Well, is he going to fix the doorknob?

MAUREEN. He's er — er —

BRIAN. What?

MAUREEN. I think you'd better go see him yourself sir.

BRIAN. I'm in the middle of a very important business discussion with Mr. Lewis. Executives can't waste their time with doorknobs. Isn't that right Sam?

SAM. You go ahead Cody I can wait.

BRIAN. No. No. Maureen can take care of this — *(He is interrupted by HOPKINS singing "Sweet Adeline." He has entered from U.L. still in his reverend outfit. He is now quite drunk.)* On second thought — *(He reacts quickly to the song and intercepts HOPKINS before he can be seen by SAM. MAUREEN exits to the office.)* Hopkins, for heaven's sake. Have you been drinking?

HOPKINS. Well sir, it's a long story.

BRIAN. We haven't got time for long stories. You have been drinking haven't you?

HOPKINS. Only water.

BRIAN. I don't believe you.

HOPKINS. It's a miracle.

BRIAN. What's a miracle?

HOPKINS. The water turned into wine.

BRIAN. Pull yourself together *(Hands him the doorknob.)* and go fix this in number seven.

HOPKINS. *(Places his hands together in a pontifical manner.)* Bless you my son.

BRIAN. Cut that out. Go and fix it or you're fired.

HOPKINS. *(To himself as he wobbles U.L., pauses to open the door of room 7, leaves it open and exits U.L.)* And you sir, are fired from my congroogiticon, congregootian, cingrogootion, er — you're fired from my flock!

BRIAN. *(Returning to his chair.)* Sorry about that. Now, where were we?

SAM. I was going to say that my wife really likes this place, but I'm beginning to have my doubts. Now, about you and Mrs. Winthrop-Smythe.

*(Enter the MAJOR, now dressed normally, from U.L. He comes R. to*

*the U.R. corner of room 7, stops and listens.)*

BRIAN. What about us?

SAM. We're going to have to break it off.

BRIAN. We are?

SAM. Yes, you see, you might feel that this is a beautiful mean-ingful relationship, *(He leans over and pats BRIAN on the knee.)* but it can't just be based on sex. *(The MAJOR reacts.)* After all, you're a married man. There's the little lady to think about.

BRIAN. No, no, you don't understand.

SAM. I understand perfectly, what I want you to understand is that you must return, both literally and figuratively, to the bosom of your wife.

BRIAN. *(Wearily.)* Right.

SAM. O.K. Now if that's understood, we can get down to busi-ness. *(The MAJOR exits U.L.)* Now, as I was saying, there's one or two things I would like to ask you.

BRIAN. Oh dear!

SAM. Firstly, why were all those people in my room and sec-ondly who, in heaven's name, was that woman with the er — er — big — er "you know whats?"

BRIAN. Ah, those. I mean her. Yes.

SAM. Yes what?

BRIAN. Yes she has big "you know whats."

SAM. I know that, I could hardly miss them. What I want to know is why was she bouncing around in my room with next to noth-ing on?

BRIAN. Bouncing?

SAM. You know what I mean. I want an explanation.

BRIAN. Well, it's a bit difficult to explain.

SAM. Try!

BRIAN. You see in this hotel we try to keep abreast of matters.

SAM. So I see.

BRIAN. You have to understand she's very patriotic.

SAM. What's that got to do with it?

BRIAN. Well, you see, she's dedicated herself to life, liberty and the happiness of pursuit.

SAM. You know Cody, sometimes you don't make a lot of sense.

BRIAN. You're the second person today who's told me that.

SAM. Is there something you're not telling me about this place?

BRIAN. There's nothing to tell. What you see is what you get. A quiet little inn in The Keys. Nothing ever happens here.

*(The door to room 6 opens and ABDUL staggers out. He is now totally disheveled, with a large bra draped over his head. He falls to his knees, staggers over to the newel post and clutches it to prevent himself falling. HAYLEY comes out wearing only a sheet wrapped around the lower half of her body and ABDUL'S burnoose covering her top. She drags him back into room 6 closing the door, watched by SAM and BRIAN.)*

SAM. *(Eventually.)* Who was that?.

BRIAN. Oh, just a couple of guests.

SAM. *(Shakes his head in bewilderment.)* That reminds me Cody. I hope you don't mind if I talk to some of your guests before I make up my mind about this place.

BRIAN. Not at all. In fact I think that's probably a very good idea. Why don't you talk to Mrs. Winthrop-Smythe? She's very knowledgeable you know. She's been coming here for years.

SAM. Has she now? You mean you and her? It's been going on for years?

BRIAN. Yes. I mean no. I mean — we're going to break it off.

SAM. I should hope so. I hope you don't mind my saying this Cody, but if I'm going to buy this place, I have to be concerned about its reputation. The owner must set the moral standard. He must be the shining example, and have you thought about what the Reverend Hopkins might say?

BRIAN. He's probably too blitzed to care.

SAM. What was that?

BRIAN. I said he probably missed his prayer.

SAM. You know, sometimes I wonder about you Cody —

*(Enter the MAJOR from U.L. He comes R. and peers cautiously around the U.R. corner of room 7. He sees SAM and BRIAN still talking.)*

MAJOR. Ahem! *(Comes down to the chairs.)*

BRIAN. *(Gets up.)* Right. I'm going to see how the doorknob is coming along. You've met the Major, haven't you?

SAM. *(Gets up to greet the MAJOR.)* Yes, of course. Why don't you sit down? We could have a little chat.

MAJOR. Splendid old chap. Nothing like a little chin-wag, what? *(They sit.)* However, I must say that I was very surprised to learn of you and Cody and your little hanky-panky-yankee. Strongly disapprove you know. Good job you broke it off. Cody should know better.

SAM. Yes, well, if you don't mind there's a couple of questions I'd like to ask you about this place.

MAJOR. Good heavens. What sort of questions?

SAM. Well, for instance, how do you find the mosquitoes here?

MAJOR. You just open the windows.

SAM. *(Pauses.)* I see. What about the food?

MAJOR. Very adequate old chap. Very adequate. I mean, perhaps a little conservative, not like some of the tucker I used to get in Africa you know. Reminds me of the time the Colonel's wife tried to make Stooky-Wooky.

SAM. Stooky-Wooky?

MAJOR. Stooky-Wooky. Terrific stuff you know.

SAM. What is it?

MAJOR. Fermented wild iguana embryo in the shell. Absolutely delicious.

SAM. *(Shudders.)* There isn't that much ketchup in the world.

MAJOR. I say old chap, you really going to buy this place?

SAM. I'm thinking about it, but there's a few things I'd like to find out about, not the least of which is what the hell you were doing in my bed?

MAJOR. Your bed old chap?

SAM. My bed.

MAJOR. Must have got the wrong room. Terribly sorry.

SAM. Well what about the other guy?

MAJOR. I thought he was with you.

SAM. Absolutely not.

MAJOR. Do you think he might have had one or two too many?

SAM. What, the Reverend?

MAJOR. It happens you know.

SAM. Yes, I suppose so, but what about the woman?

MAJOR. Ah yes. *(Thoughtful.)* The woman. Which woman?

SAM. You know. The one with the big — wait a minute — let's do this a different way. The one with no clothes.

MAJOR. I thought that was your wife.

SAM. Well, my wife doesn't have any clothes, but I meant the other woman.

MAJOR. You mean, as well as Mr. Cody and your wife, there's another woman in your life?

SAM. There's no other woman in my life. I mean the other woman in my room. Oh, what's the use, the one with the big "you know whats."

MAJOR. Big "you know whats?" Oh, I see, you mean "gesumbahs." You must mean Miss Harrington.

SAM. Right.

MAJOR. Right. *(Pause.)* What was your question again?

SAM. What was she doing?

MAJOR. Well, she kept opening her robe, old chap.

SAM. I know that. I was there. But why?

MAJOR. Haven't the faintest idea. *(He gets up.)* I've got to be going. If you're going to buy this place, you should remember what was said in 1776. "Indubitus Miseratus."

SAM. Who was it said that?

MAJOR. I've no idea. Some fool who couldn't speak English I suppose. Cheerio old chap.

*(The MAJOR exits jauntily to the front entrance. Enter U.L. BRIAN and HOPKINS, still in his reverend outfit, but carrying his tool box.)*

BRIAN. Just put the damn thing back on please.

HOPKINS. There's no need to be rude.

*(HOPKINS works on the door while Brian comes R. and sits with SAM.)*

BRIAN. Now, where were we?

SAM. Well now, I've had a little chat with the Major. He seems to have cleared up one or two things. You know Cody, I'm beginning to feel a little better about this place. Earlier this afternoon I was beginning to think you were running some sort of weird bordello or something.

BRIAN. Bordello here? I can't imagine where you would get such a strange idea.

SAM. Well, I can't imagine either. Perhaps it's because someone in this hotel is determined to keep my wife in a state of permanent undress. A mad Major and a tipsy clergyman crawl into my bed in their underwear, while Miss Twin Peaks cavorts around the room defying gravity. Did I mention you and your affair with the Palm Beach country club?

BRIAN. Ah yes! I can see how you might have misinterpreted a few things.

SAM. Well, now that everybody seems to be wearing clothes again, I'm prepared to accept that everything was just a misunderstanding. So — we'll get down to business — *(He stands.)* If you'll excuse me, I was making some notes during the flight to Miami.

They're in my briefcase in the car. I'll just go and get them.

*(Exits front entrance. The following action occurs almost simultane-
ously in a very rapid sequence:*

  *1. TERRI and ASHLEY come down the stairs. ASHLEY is
still wearing her towel, and TERRI carries yet another dress.
They come just below the last step.*

  *2. BRIAN gets up from the chair and turns U.S. toward
TERRI and ASHLEY.*

  *3. HOPKINS, quite drunk, comes R. along the hall singing
"Sweet Adeline."*

  *4. The door of room 6 opens, ABDUL runs out and bumps
into TERRI who, trying to save her balance, grabs ASHLEY'S
towel. ASHLEY and TERRI both scream.*

  *5. BRIAN, seeing the towel about to be pulled off ASHLEY,
leaps to the rescue and ends up holding the towel to hide her.*

  *6. TERRI falls down on her back with ABDUL kneeling
astride her in a suggestive position.*

  *7. HAYLEY comes charging out of room 6, runs straight
into HOPKINS. Her momentum carries them both to the chairs
where HOPKINS falls over backward, his legs in the air with
HAYLEY on top of him.*

  *8. MAUREEN, hearing the screams, now in her receptionist
outfit but minus the skirt, runs out of the office and comes L. of
the counter.*

*SAM enters from the front entrance carrying a briefcase. He pauses,
looks at the incredible scene in front of him and half turns to the
audience.)*

SAM. I knew it! It's the best little fun house in Florida.


**(The curtain falls.)**

### Scene 2

*(Later the same evening. The bed in room 7 has been made and all bottles, glasses, etc., have been removed. BRIAN and TERRI are sitting in the two chairs.)*

BRIAN. Well, we finally got everybody calmed down.

TERRI. I told you everything would turn out just fine.

BRIAN. Nothing has "turned out." We're absolutely no further ahead than when we started, and Mr. Lewis still hasn't made an offer on this place.

TERRI. Oh Brian, we're a lot further ahead. For starters we've sorted out the mix up with room seven. The Lewises have it to themselves. The Barracuda very graciously agreed to move to number nine. We've found Mrs. Lewis' clothes, though I still don't know how they ended up in the office, and we've got everybody safely into dinner.

BRIAN. Not everybody. The Major and the Barracuda are still missing.

TERRI. You know, I've hardly seen her since she got here. The Major must be doing a great job.

BRIAN. Well, I just wish he'd stop playing at Lawrence of Arabia.

*(Enter MAUREEN from the front entrance. She is in her receptionist outfit.)*

MAUREEN. Excuse me Mrs. Cody, but you're needed in the kitchen.

TERRI. Thanks Maureen. *(She stands up.)* By the way, let's have no more confusion about rooms. The next available one is number six. As soon as you get a chance make sure it's all made up. You know the routine, clean sheets, towels, check the bathroom.

MAUREEN. I'm the maid again?

TERRI. I'm afraid so.

*(MAUREEN starts to run into the office.)*

BRIAN. Hold it a second. *(MAUREEN stops and turns.)* There's one other thing Maureen. As soon as dinner is finished I'm going to try to get Mr. Lewis alone in here to talk business and he'll probably be ordering after-dinner drinks.

MAUREEN. Yes sir.

BRIAN. Now, as you know. I'm not a very good drinker and I'm determined to keep my wits about me this evening. So when we order drinks I'll say to you "my usual please." When you serve the drinks, you give him whatever he ordered, but you'll pass me water. Do you understand?

MAUREEN. Yes sir. I think so. When you ask me for a drink, I pass water!

TERRI. *(Laughing.)* Good luck Brian. Come on. I'm needed in the kitchen and you really ought to get back to the dining room.

*(TERRI and BRIAN exit to the front entrance. MAUREEN sprints into the office. The door of number 6 opens and ABDUL staggers out. He comes down and flops into one of the chairs.)*

ABDUL. I must take a break!

HAYLEY. *(Appears in the doorway in her robe.)* Well if you must, you must, but it seems like such a waste of time. *(ABDUL groans.)* Oh, alright. I know, you need food. Give me a minute while I get dressed and we'll go and have some dinner. Then afterwards, we can really get down to some serious activity. *(ABDUL groans and slumps in the chair. HAYLEY comes down and peers at him over the back of the chair.)* That's funny, you look quite different upside down. Ooh — that gives me an idea. *(ABDUL groans.)* Won't be a minute.

*(Exits to room 6 and closes the door. Enter HOPKINS from the front entrance. He sees ABDUL, who has closed his eyes, comes over to him and examines his face very carefully.)*

HOPKINS. It's amazing!

ABDUL. I know. I don't know how she does it.

HOPKINS. No. I mean you. You look just like the Major.

ABDUL. So I understand, but right now I'm too exhausted to care. I don't think I can keep it up much longer.

HOPKINS. What you need is a little "pick me up." *(He looks around, then goes to the newel post and starts to unscrew the knob.)* By the way, my name is Hopkins.

ABDUL. I am Abdul El Hajj. I used to be known as the Lion of the Desert. What on earth are you doing?

HOPKINS. *(Turning the knob.)* You'll see in a minute.

*(MAUREEN, now in her maid's outfit, runs out of the office past HOPKINS and exits U.L.)*

ABDUL. The women in this hotel — they all seem so — so active.

*(HOPKINS now has unscrewed the knob, reached down inside and produced a bottle of liquor and two small glasses. He replaces the knob, brings the bottle and glasses down to the two chairs and pours two generous shots.)*

HOPKINS. Here. *(Hands ABDUL a glass.)* Try a drop of this. It'll put you back on your feet in no time.

ABDUL. *(Looking at his glass.)* It's not alcoholic is it?

HOPKINS. Well, no, not very much.

ABDUL. *(Suspiciously.)* Well, what is it?

HOPKINS. It's — er — er Polish mineral water — yes that's it, Polish mineral water.

ABDUL. Is it good for you?

HOPKINS. Are you kidding? It's wonderful. *(He raises his glass.)* Well, bottoms up!

ABDUL. Not for a little while I hope, I need the rest.

*(He drinks.)*

HOPKINS. *(Pouring two more shots.)* There's nothing like a drop of mineral water.

ABDUL. *(Shaking his head.)* It certainly appears to have great restorative qualities.

*(He drinks again.)*

HAYLEY. *(Enters from room 6, now dressed and carrying her suitcase.)* Ah! The Reverend!

HOPKINS. *(Jumps up and rushes to her side.)* I am at your service Madam.

HAYLEY. That's nice! *(She runs her fingers suggestively around his collar and then down the front of his shirt.)* Because he *(Nodding to ABDUL who has slumped down in his chair again and closed his eyes.)* looks like he's had it — at least for a while. *(Aside to HOPKINS:)* Why don't you meet me in my new room later. It's number nine. *(To ABDUL:)* I'll just put my case away and I'll be right back.

*(She exits U.L.)*

HOPKINS. *(Rubbing his hands together in anticipation.)* Right. Number nine.

ABDUL. Could I please have some more of that mineral water?

HOPKINS. *(Pours another shot.)* Why not?

ABDUL. What about you?

*(MAUREEN enters U. L. with towels, etc., comes R. and exits to room 6.)*

HOPKINS. Well, under normal circumstances, I would, but now things have changed. I've got to stay sober, my ship is about to come in. I've got to stay fit for later.

ABDUL. What's that?

HOPKINS. I said I've got to go and tip the waiter. Yes, that's it. I need coffee. I'll leave you the rest of the — er — mineral water. You look like you could use it.

*(Exit front entrance. Enter HAYLEY from U.L. She comes R. and sits next to ABDUL.)*

HAYLEY. I thought you didn't drink.

ABDUL. Oh, I don't. This is Polish mineral water. Would you care for some?

HAYLEY. No thanks. Do you mind if I ask you a question?

ABDUL. You want to talk?

HAYLEY. Well, yes.

ABDUL. That makes a change.

HAYLEY. You're allowed to have four wives right?

ABDUL. Not you as well. What is this Western fixation with an old, and mostly discontinued, custom?

HAYLEY. Well, what I wondered was — well — you know — if you had four wives, how would they manage — you know — about sex?

ABDUL. Ah! I see. Well. Infrequently.

HAYLEY. *(Thinks for a moment.)* Is that one word or two?

ABDUL. For your information, I don't even have one wife.

HAYLEY. Really. Why not?

ABDUL. Well I don't want to get tied down.

HAYLEY. Shame! I kinda like that kinky stuff. *(She gets up.)* Come on. Lets get something to eat and recharge our batteries.

*(ABDUL groans again as they exit to the front entrance. MAUREEN comes out of room 6, closes the door, picks up the bottle and two glasses and heads for the office as DOROTHY enters from the front entrance. She is a large woman, age about 50. She carries a*

*suitcase and a large rolled umbrella. Dressed very severely in a dark, matron-like suit, with flat shoes and hat. In manner, bearing and looks she is best described as "an old battleaxe.")*

DOROTHY. Here. You!

MAUREEN. *(Stops and puts the bottle and glasses down on the counter.)* Me?

DOROTHY. Of course you. You don't see anyone else do you?

MAUREEN. Well, no —

DOROTHY. I understand my husband checked in here today. I'd like you to show me to our room.

*(She runs her finger along the counter, checking for dust, then looks at her finger with an expression of total disgust.)*

MAUREEN. Your husband?

DOROTHY. Yes. My husband. Samuel B. Lewis.

MAUREEN. I thought it was only Sheiks who could have more than one wife.

DOROTHY. What's that? Speak up girl.

MAUREEN. He can't be your husband. He's married.

DOROTHY. Of course he's married. Has been for twenty-three years. Now which room is he in?

MAUREEN. I think he's in the dining room.

DOROTHY. You stupid girl. I meant — oh never mind. I'll freshen up and join him. What's our room number?

MAUREEN. You mean Mr. Lewis's.

DOROTHY. Of course, Mr. Lewis's.

MAUREEN. It's number seven.

DOROTHY. Well don't just stand there, pick up my case and show me where it is.

*(MAUREEN does so and leads DOROTHY U.L. She opens the door of*

*number 7. DOROTHY strides past her into the room, pokes the bed with her umbrella, checks for dust on the table then opens the bathroom door. She turns to MAUREEN.)*

DOROTHY. This room is not satisfactory. The toilet is running. What sort of hotel is this? Find me another room immediately.

*(She marches out past MAUREEN and comes R.)*

MAUREEN. *(Running after her with the suitcase.)* That would be number six.

*(DOROTHY stops, sees the number, then marches straight in. MAUREEN waits outside, mimics her walk and raises her eyes to the heavens.)*

DOROTHY. *(Reappearing.)* It's a miserable pokey little room, but I suppose it will have to do.

*(She grabs the suitcase, goes into the room and slams the door. The number six is flipped down and now reads number nine. MAUREEN returns to behind the counter as the MAJOR enters from the front entrance.)*

MAUREEN. Good evening Major.
MAJOR. Ah, Maureen. Good evening. I wonder if I might elicit a little confidential information from you.
MAUREEN. What?
MAJOR. I'd like to ask you a question.
MAUREEN. O.K.
MAJOR. Now that you've got all the rooms straightened out, could you tell me which room is Miss Harrington's?
MAUREEN. Oh sure. *(She looks at the board.)* She's in number nine.

MAJOR. Thank you. Frightfully good of you old girl. Jolly good show. Number nine.

*(He turns to go U.L.)*

MAUREEN. Have fun Major!

MAJOR. *(Comes back R.)* Now you do understand that all this is in the line of duty?

MAUREEN. *(Teasing.)* Of course Major. What else could it be?

MAJOR. Right. As long as that's clearly understood. Goodnight.

MAUREEN. Goodnight. *(She pauses as the Major turns U.L. again.)* Don't let the Barracuda bite.

*(She bursts into a fit of giggles.)*

MAJOR. *(Turns back R.)* Let me assure you that your pathetic little attempt at jocularity will definitely fall on deaf ears. I shall do my duty. *(He turns again and winks at the audience.)*

MAUREEN. *(Salutes.)* We, who are about to die — laughing — salute you.

MAJOR. Right. Number nine.

*(He goes U.L., stops at the door of number six, does a double-take at the number nine, shrugs his shoulders and goes in closing the door. There is a piercing yell, then the door is flung open. The MAJOR races out followed by DOROTHY. She is in her underwear, which is the most unglamorous ensemble imaginable. It consists of bloomers reaching below the knees and a massive long-line corset-bra. She chases him U.L. a few steps with her upraised umbrella till he disappears from sight, then turns and sees MAUREEN, who has been watching in amusement from behind the counter.)*

DOROTHY What sort of a place are you running here? I was almost raped in my own room. Just wait till my husband hears about this. Really!

*(She re-enters room six and closes the door. Enter HOPKINS from the front entrance. He nods at MAUREEN as he goes past her and goes U.L. He stops outside number 6, does a double-take at the 9, primps, waves to MAUREEN and enters the room. MAUREEN counts silently to the audience, "one, two, three." HOPKINS re-appears with an agonizing yell, followed by DOROTHY and her upraised umbrella. He escapes U.L.)*

DOROTHY. This place is nothing but a den of iniquity. That clergyman grabbed me by the buttocks. I've never been so humiliated in my life. The management will definitely hear about this.

*(She goes back in room 6 and closes the door. HOPKINS creeps back D.R., grabs the "Polish mineral water" off the counter and runs back U.L. MAUREEN shrugs at the audience as ABDUL runs in . from the front entrance looking over his shoulder.)*

ABDUL. I'm going to my room to rest. If Miss Harrington wants me, please, please, don't tell her where I am.

*(He goes straight to room 6.)*

MAUREEN. I don't think your room is —

*(ABDUL is now in room 6. MAUREEN does her "one, two, three" routine. The door of room 6 is flung open, ABDUL crawls out on his knees. DOROTHY is beating him with her umbrella.)*

DOROTHY. Take that, you brute. And that, you monster. You men are all alike. Licentious beasts. All of you.

*(She goes back in room 6 and slams the door.)*

ABDUL. *(From the floor.)* Dear mother of a she-camel. What was that?

MAUREEN. Probably the mother of a she-camel.

ABDUL. I'll tell you one thing. If she lived in India, she'd be sacred! *(Getting up.)* I need some more of that Polish mineral water. I must find the Reverend.

*(He staggers off U. L. Enter from the entrance, BRIAN, TERRI, SAM and ASHLEY.)*

BRIAN. I'm so glad you enjoyed your dinner.

SAM. Just excellent Cody. Perhaps we should continue our little discussion over an after-dinner drink.

TERRI. I think I'll just go upstairs and get all those clothes back in Mrs. Cody's closet.

*(She exits upstairs.)*

ASHLEY. And I'm going to go and sit on the patio while you guys talk business. It's such a beautiful night. See you later honey.

*(She gives SAM a peck on the cheek, goes up to room 7, enters, closes the door and exits through the French windows.)*

BRIAN. *(Motions to SAM to sit in the chairs.)* Now Maureen, we'd like a little drink please. What would you like Sam?

SAM. A small brandy would be nice. Thank you.

BRIAN. Right. A brandy for Mr. Lewis, Maureen, and *(Winks at her.)* I'll have my usual.

MAUREEN. Your usual what sir?

BRIAN. You know. My usual!

MAUREEN. Oh, I remember. Yes sir. Your usual.

*(She rushes off U.L.)*

BRIAN. Where are you going? The bar's that way.

*(He points to the front entrance.)*

MAUREEN. I know sir, but first I'm going to the bathroom. Don't you remember you told me —
BRIAN. Yes, O.K. I remember. Carry on Maureen.
MAUREEN. Yes sir.

*(She exits U.L.)*

SAM. Now Cody, before we talk business, there's still one or two things I'd like to clear up. I hope you won't consider these questions too personal, but I do need to get the feel of the place.
BRIAN. Personal?
SAM. Yes. For example, are you quite sure that you and Mrs. Winthrop-Smythe have finished your affair?
BRIAN. Oh yes! Our affair is over. Definitely.
SAM. That's good. *(MAUREEN comes back down R. BRIAN gets up.)* Because if it became known, this hotel could acquire a very unsavory reputation. *(BRIAN is not really listening, but indicating to MAUREEN that she shouldn't be in her maid's outfit. He ushers her into the office not really hearing SAM'S next words.)* All right, we'll let it drop, now on to more practical matters. What about vacations? It must be very difficult for you to get away. *(MAUREEN exits to the office, BRIAN once again paying attention, returns to his chair.)* Just how often do you and Mrs. Cody do it?
BRIAN. *(He pauses with eyes bulging.)* Do it?
SAM. Yes. How often? And do you do it together or do you go

off separately? *(He pauses. BRIAN is speechless.)* I also need to know what time of year you find best for it?

BRIAN. What?

SAM. Yes. You see Mrs. Lewis and I make a point of doing it once every summer, and we also try very hard to do it a second time in the middle of winter.

BRIAN. Twice a year?

SAM. Yes. We are very fortunate aren't we. Frankly, I don't see how you and Mrs. Cody can possibly do it at all.

BRIAN. I can assure you —

SAM. It must be difficult for you, believe me I know how hard it is to find good help these days.

BRIAN. You need help?

SAM. Don't look so surprised. We all need help you know. *(BRIAN is shaking his head in disbelief.)* Anyway it's not important. Now about the hotel. I see your asking price on the listing, and frankly it seems just a little high to me.

BRIAN. Well, it might appear that way, but if you take into consideration —

*(DOROTHY has come out of room 6. She is now dressed but still carrying her umbrella. Both men look over their shoulders.)*

DOROTHY. Samuel!

SAM. *(Jumps to his feet and goes to her.)* Dorothy! What are you doing here?

DOROTHY. Well, my Bible conference was cancelled, and your secretary told me where you were. You know I wanted to see this place, especially as you were thinking of buying it. So I caught the next plane down. However, I must say, that so far, it has met with my severe disapproval. There appear to be bunches of men running around with their hormones hanging out. *(She appears to notice BRIAN for the first time.)* Who's this? *(She points and almost prods him with her umbrella.)*

SAM. This is Mr. Cody. He's the owner of the Turtle Beach Hotel.

BRIAN. *(Offers his hand.)* How do you do? You must be — er — er — er —

DOROTHY. *(Disdaining his hand.)* Mrs. Lewis.

BRIAN. I see, Mrs. Lewis. As in the wife of Mr. Lewis.

DOROTHY. Of course. And I want you to know, young man, that my husband will not be buying this hotel unless I approve of it, and so far I do not!

SAM. In that case my dear, I don't think you should stay here. Why don't I take you to another hotel?

DOROTHY. Nonsense. Why would you want to go to another hotel?

SAM. Well — er — er — it's not good enough for you my sweet.

DOROTHY. Don't be ridiculous. How can we find out if we want to buy it if we don't stay here.

BRIAN. You're Mrs. Lewis?

DOROTHY. *(To SAM.)* Is he a little slow or something?

SAM. Well, er —

DOROTHY. The maid told me you've had dinner so we'll just go and have dessert and coffee in the dining room, and then straight to our room for an early night.

SAM. Our room?

DOROTHY. Yes. This one. *(Indicates room 6.)* It's small and pokey , and not nearly as nice as the one you were in, number seven, but the toilet was running in there.

BRIAN. I can get that fixed.

SAM. *(Glares at BRIAN.)* No, no. Don't bother. We don't want number seven. We'll be just fine in here in number six.

DOROTHY. No we won't. Young man, that's the first good thing I've heard about this place. While we're in the dining room, fix the toilet and get the maid to move my things into number seven. Come along Samuel.

*(She starts to drag a reluctant SAM off toward the front entrance. SAM looks helplessly at BRIAN who comes D.R. with them.)*

BRIAN. Don't you worry about a thing Mrs. Lewis. I'll even take care of those men you were worried about. *(Enjoying himself now.)* After all we don't approve of any hanky-panky in this hotel, do we Mr. Lewis?

SAM. *(Squirming.)* No. Of course not.

BRIAN. We must control our animal impulses. Right Mr. Lewis?

SAM. Er — right.

BRIAN. *(On a roll now.)* We have to worry about the reputation of the place. The owner must set the moral standard. He must be the shining example. Right Mr. Lewis?

SAM. Er — right.

BRIAN. Good. I'll get our maintenance man right away.

DOROTHY. Come along Samuel.

SAM. *(Desperate.)* Er — there's one thing Mr. Cody.

BRIAN. Yes, Mr. Lewis?

SAM. I've been thinking, you know, about our business, and — er — in the light of — er — what you told me, I think the previous asking price, plus fifty thousand would be about right, if — er —, you know, — things were to work out.

DOROTHY. For heaven's sake Samuel. Come along. We'll talk business tomorrow.

*(DOROTHY exits front entrance.)*

SAM. *(Almost under his breath.)* Coming my little piranha fish.

*(SAM exits front entrance.)*

BRIAN. *(Does a little skip and starts moving rapidly in circles.)* Asking price plus fifty thousand — plus fifty thousand, Wow! *(Calms down just a little bit.)* If things work out. *(Rushes U.L.)* Fix the toilet. *(Stops.)* The first Mrs. Lewis, she can't see her, so, — don't fix the toilet. No, she says this room *(Indicates room 6.)* is pokey. *(Snaps his fingers.)* I've got it. Fix the toilet and move the first Mrs. Lewis out of number seven. That's it. I can do all this on my own. I can just see Terri at breakfast tomorrow. I'll say "Good morning dear. Oh, by the way, I sold the hotel last night. Here's the check. You'll notice it's for a few pennies more than we were asking. The negotiations were tough, but then tough is my middle name." *(MAUREEN enters from the office with two drinks on a tray. She is now in her room service outfit.)* Maureen. Where's Hopkins?

MAUREEN. Last time I saw him he was in the laundry room with that Arab Sheik, sitting on top of a dryer, singing "The hills are alive with the waters of Poland."

BRIAN. Get him quickly. Tell him the toilet's running in number seven. He's got to fix it.

MAUREEN. What about the drinks?

BRIAN. *(Takes the tray from her and puts it on the counter.)* We won't need them now. Get Hopkins, quickly, please.

*(MAUREEN hurries off U.L.)*

TERRI. *(Coming down the stairs.)* Oh, there you are. Where's Mr. Lewis? Have you finished talking? Did he make an offer?

BRIAN. *(Trying to act casual.)* Not yet. He's gone back to the dining room for coffee.

TERRI. Well, did he say anything?

BRIAN. Not too much. The negotiations were tough.

TERRI. *(Horrified.)* What negotiations?

BRIAN. Well, you know.

TERRI. No. I don't know.

BRIAN. I think —

TERRI. I don't want you to think dear. That's when we always get into trouble. Just remember, we'll come down $100,000 from the asking price, no more. That's what we decided.

BRIAN. Leave it to me, my love.

TERRI. That's the problem. This time I'm afraid I'm going to have to.


*(She looks around to make sure no one is watching, then gives him a little kiss and exits to the front entrance. Enter from U.L. ABDUL and HOPKINS. They are clearly drunk. They sway down the hall, arms around each other, ABDUL carries the tool box. They are followed by MAUREEN. BRIAN rushes L. to meet them.)*

BRIAN. *(To ABDUL:)* What the hell are you doing here? Oh never mind. There's no time. *(They are between the doors of rooms 6 and 8.)* Wait here. *(He goes to room 7, knocks then opens the door.)* Hello. Anyone in? Mrs. Lewis? *(Looks down the hall.)* Good. Now Hopkins, fix the toilet.

HOPKINS. *(Entering room 7, followed by ABDUL.)* Have you met my new astitant? My new ashishant? My helper?

ABDUL. SHANGO PITHNA MONSANKO MOR.

HOPKINS. What did he say?

BRIAN. I can't believe it matters. For heaven's sake, just get going.

*(HOPKINS and ABDUL both step into the bathroom doorway. They wedge together. They struggle for a moment then ABDUL slides slowly down the doorframe and remains sitting on the floor in a motionless stupor. HOPKINS enters the bathroom. BRIAN returns to the hall and leads MAUREEN, who has been watching, from the door of 7, to room 6.)*

BRIAN. Now. In here. *(He opens the door of room 6.)* Pack all the clothes in here in the suitcase, then come and get me.

*(MAUREEN goes into room 6 and closes the door. Enter SAM, running through the front entrance.)*

SAM. Cody, you've got to help me. I meant what I said. Fifty thousand extra.

BRIAN. What am I supposed to do about the first Mrs. Lewis?

SAM. Put her in another room. Remove all traces of her in number seven. Just don't let my wife see her, she'll kill me.

BRIAN. Yes, she probably would. How long have you been married to her?

SAM. Since 1859! I've got to get back. Don't let me down Cody. Remember, fifty thousand.

*(SAM exits front entrance.)*

BRIAN. *(Goes to room 7 and calls as he comes down to the door.)* How's it going?

HOPKINS. *(Comes out of the bathroom.)* All fixed, no problem.

BRIAN. How could you fix it so quickly?

HOPKINS. *(To the audience.)* It's my pension plan again.

BRIAN. Right. Let's go. Hurry. *(He takes a quick look down the hall to make sure the coast is clear, then comes back in the room.)* What about him? *(Pointing to ABDUL.)* He can't stay there. Here, give me a hand.

*(They get him to his feet.)*

ABDUL. I think I need some more mineral water.

HOPKINS. *(Supporting ABDUL as they sway R. along the hall.)* That's right. Mineral water. I have some more upstairs.

ABDUL. May Allah bless the waters of Poland!

*(They get just past room 8 when HOPKINS stops and removes the bottle of wine from the still life painting. They exit upstairs singing. BRIAN has picked up the toolbox, closed the bathroom door, looked in the dressing room, closed the door, exited room 7, closed the door, and exited U.L.*
*Enter ASHLEY from the patio. She goes into the dressing room. BRIAN enters U.L. now minus the toolbox. He runs down to the front entrance and looks out. He rubs his hands together.)*

BRIAN. So far, so good. Fix the toilet. That's done. Now what's next? Move Mrs. Lewis. Remove all traces of her in number seven.

*(Enter MAUREEN from room 6, DOROTHY'S suitcase in her hand. BRIAN sees her and comes U.S.)*

MAUREEN. What do you want me to do with these clothes?
BRIAN. They're going in room seven. But not for a minute. Just put them down for a second and follow me. *(MAUREEN puts the case down. ASHLEY, now wearing a floral lace teddy, comes out of the dressing room, closes the door and goes into the bathroom, closing the door. BRIAN, followed by MAUREEN, knocks on the door of number 7. There is no answer so he opens the door.)* Hello, Mrs. Lewis? Right Maureen. *(He opens the dressing room door.)* Take all the female clothing out of here and put it in number six.
MAUREEN. *(Going into the dressing room.)* There's something real kinky going on here.
BRIAN. Just do it please.
*(He runs down the hall and nearly bumps into the MAJOR who has entered from the front entrance)*

MAJOR. I say steady on old chap.
BRIAN. Oh. Sorry Major.
MAJOR. You look really frazzled old chap. Is there something I

can do?

BRIAN. *(Moving in circles again.)* Move Mrs. Lewis. Move Mrs. Lewis.

MAJOR. You feeling alright old chap? Got a touch of the sun have we? I remember once, up the river Bangala, come to think of it I didn't have a paddle.

BRIAN. No, it's alright Major, you've done enough, you've kept your part of the bargain. You've kept the Barracuda busy all day.

MAJOR. Well, actually old chap, I was going to talk to you about that. I haven't done anything you see.

BRIAN. *(Not really listening.)* Move Mrs. Lewis. Where the hell is Mrs. Lewis?

MAJOR. Who?

BRIAN. Mrs. Lewis.

MAJOR. Oh, the one without clothes.

BRIAN. Well, she's not really Mrs. Lewis. She's just the first Mrs. Lewis. Then there's the second Mrs. Lewis, but she was in six *(Looks at door.)* I mean nine — well it's supposed to be six.

MAJOR. Mrs. Lewis?

BRIAN. Yes.

MAJOR. In there?

BRIAN. For heaven's sake yes.

MAJOR. I thought it was a manatee!

BRIAN. What?

MAJOR. I thought I'd been attacked by a rabid manatee.

BRIAN. That's Mrs. Lewis.

MAJOR. She's about as friendly as a dyspeptic puff-adder.

BRIAN. That's the one.

MAJOR. Something happen to her? A fatal accident perhaps?

BRIAN. No, nothing happened to her, but that was the real Mrs. Lewis.

MAJOR. You mean the first one, the one with no clothes was — er — not Mrs. Lewis?

BRIAN. That's right.

MAJOR. Good show old chap. You've got him then.

BRIAN. What do you mean?

MAJOR. You've got him by the short ones old chap.

BRIAN. Yes, I suppose I do, don't I.

MAJOR. No doubt about it. You can sell him this place for any price you want.

BRIAN. I can?

MAJOR. Of course. Remember what one of your former presidents said, "Once you've got them by the balls, their hearts and minds quickly follow."

BRIAN. Whatever happens, the second Mrs. Lewis mustn't find the first one. You understand?

MAJOR. "The second Mrs. Lewis mustn't find the first one." Got it. You can count on me old chap.

*(MAUREEN has come out of the dressing room with a bundle of clothes over her arm. She accidentally drops a black lace bra on the floor, just inside the door of room 7 and then comes R.)*

BRIAN. *(Rushes to meet her.)* Right, put those in here.

*(He opens the door of room 6.)*

MAUREEN. There's definitely something kinky going on.

*(She exits to room 6.)*

BRIAN. *(Closes the door of room 6.)* Where the hell is Mrs. Lewis?

MAJOR. The one without clothes or the manatee?

BRIAN. The one without clothes — except she's got clothes. The patio! She said she'd be on the patio.

*(He is about to turn to go to room 7, but stops dead in his tracks as he sees SAM and DOROTHY enter from the front entrance.)*

MAJOR. *(His back to SAM and DOROTHY.)* You know old chap that woman in there *(Indicates room 6.)* sounded like a walrus being machine-gunned. That women is a lunatic, that woman is insane, that woman is a threat to the entire human race, that woman is standing right behind me isn't she?

DOROTHY. *(Ignoring the MAJOR and pointing to BRIAN, who is trying to escape, with her umbrella.)* Where do you think you're going?

BRIAN. Well I —

DOROTHY. Have you packed my clothes?

*(She points at the suitcase with her umbrella.)*

BRIAN. Well I —

DOROTHY. Who is this?

*(She prods the MAJOR with her umbrella.)*

BRIAN. This is —

DOROTHY. You're not one of those creatures who assaulted me are you?

MAJOR. I can assure you madam I—

DOROTHY. I should hope not. Mr. Cody, show us to our room. You! *(She prods the MAJOR again.)* Bring my case.

*(BRIAN rushes ahead to room 7. SAM, DOROTHY and the MAJOR, carrying the suitcase, all follow. BRIAN tries to get to the patio but doesn't quite make it. He is just outside the bathroom door when:)*

DOROTHY. *(In a voice that could be heard in Miami.)* What is this?

*(She has picked up the bra with the end of her umbrella and come down to the end of the bed, followed by SAM. The MAJOR is in the doorway. She holds it triumphantly aloft.)*

MAJOR. *(Puts down the case and takes a step into the room.)* Actually it's a —

DOROTHY. I know what it is. What I want to know is, whose is it?

*(Before anyone can answer, that bathroom door opens and ASHLEY appears briefly. BRIAN closes the door with a bang.)*

DOROTHY. What was that?

BRIAN. *(Keeps his hand on the doorknob to prevent ASHLEY from opening it and stamps his foot.)* Termites. Nasty little things. *(He stamps his foot again. DOROTHY looks away, ASHLEY bangs on the door. As DOROTHY turns to BRIAN he bangs on the door with the palm of his hand.)* There goes another one. *(He stamps again, several times, ending with a classic Spanish dancer's pose with one arm above his head.)* Ole!

DOROTHY. *(Looks at BRIAN for a moment.)* I'm waiting for an explanation as to why this — this — thing, this lewd, licentious, lascivious —

SAM. For heaven's sake Dorothy, it's a bra!

DOROTHY. But it's black, and it's frilly, it's disgusting. *(She lowers the umbrella a little.)* Here get rid of it. *(SAM goes to reach for it.)* Not you Samuel. Don't touch it. It might set you off. Here Mr. Cody.

*(BRIAN lets go of the bathroom door and comes U.S. to take the bra. ASHLEY opens the bathroom door and steps into the room. She is still in her teddy.)*

DOROTHY. Oh, I think I am going to faint.

*(She sits on the bed.)*

ASHLEY. Sam, what's going on here?
DOROTHY. *(Recovering fast.)* Who is this woman?

*(There is a long silence. SAM looks at BRIAN who looks desperately at the MAJOR.)*

MAJOR. This is my wife.

*(He strides D.S., grabs ASHLEY before she can say anything and gives her a big kiss, full on the lips.)*

SAM. *(Grinning at BRIAN.)* That's the Major's wife.
ASHLEY. *(Manages to get her lips free.)* What in heaven's name —

*(The MAJOR kisses her again. They all watch.)*

SAM. Yes sir. That's the Major's wife.
ASHLEY. *(Comes up for air.)* Will somebody please —

*(The MAJOR kisses her again.)*

DOROTHY. *(Yelling.)* She's naked.
SAM. She has trouble with clothes.
ASHLEY. *(She and the MAJOR break apart a little and in a much quieter voice.)* Oh my goodness Major.

*(She gazes into his eyes.)*

BRIAN. *(Still holding the bra, turns to go.)* Well, I think I'll just be running along.

*(He turns L. and now has his back to DOROTHY.)*

DOROTHY. You're not going anywhere, *(Holding her umbrella by the tip she swings it in a vicious uppercut motion. The umbrella goes between his legs from the rear finishing with the handle hooked between his legs. BRIAN collapses with a groan.)* until I have an explanation for the presence of this woman in my bathroom.

ASHLEY. Your bathroom! Why, I'll have you know —

*(The MAJOR kisses her again.)*

SAM. *(Starts to propel ASHLEY and the MAJOR toward the door.)* Come along you two. I think they just got the wrong room dear.

ASHLEY. *(Dreamily.)* Well then, let's find another one.

*(She gazes into the MAJOR'S eyes and snuggles up on his shoulder.)*

MAJOR. Right Ho. Jolly good show, what?

ASHLEY. Jolly good show.

*(They wander straight into room 8, arm in arm, unable to take their eyes off each other.)*

SAM. *(Looking at BRIAN on the floor.)* I don't think you should have done that dear.

DOROTHY. Is he alright?

*(BRIAN groans.)*

SAM. I think so. *(He helps BRIAN up, who now stands with his legs well apart.)* I think you should apologize dear. After all, Mr. Cody was just doing his job.

DOROTHY. Apologize? I shall do no such thing. This place is a disgrace. I had no sooner got here than I was assaulted by someone whose face I couldn't see, then by a man I could have sworn was a member of the clergy, and finally by the Sheik of Araby. I arrive in this room to find underthings scattered all over the floor, there are termites crawling through the walls, a half-naked woman comes out of the bathroom and practically starts to fornicate with that suspicious looking character, and you want me to apologize.

BRIAN. Madam, I can assure you —

DOROTHY. The only thing you can be assured of, is that under no circumstances, and not for any price will I permit Samuel to purchase this — this den of depravity.

BRIAN. So that's that then.

*(ABDUL and HOPKINS have entered at the top of the stairs. They are very drunk, leaning on each other and swaying dangerously. They are singing " The Wiffenpoof Song.")*

ABDUL and HOPKINS.
"We're poor little lambs who have lost our way"

*(BRIAN comes R. and stands just U.S. of the chairs. DOROTHY and SAM follow and come to the U.R. corner of room 7.)*

ABDUL and HOPKINS.
"Baaa, baaa, baaa."

*(MAUREEN opens the door of room 6 and steps out. TERRI and HAYLEY enter from the front entrance and stop D.R.)*

ABDUL and HOPKINS.
"We're little black sheep who have gone astray.
Baaa, baaa, baaa."

DOROTHY. *(Raising her umbrella.)* It's them!

*(Startled, ABDUL falls, HOPKINS tries unsuccessfully to catch him.*

*Everybody screams. He rolls all the way down and comes to a stop at the foot of the stairs. [See author's note.] His head, covered by the burnoose, faces upstage.)*

MAUREEN. *(She is the first one there. She kneels and places ABDUL'S head in her lap.)* Oh my God.

TERRI. *(Rushes up.)* Is he alright?

MAUREEN. I think so. Yes, he's coming around. *(Everyone has crowded around.)* Give him some air. *(Everyone backs away a little.)* Yes, he's moving.

HAYLEY. *(Comes U.S.)* Well, as long as he's alright. How about it Reverend?

HOPKINS. *(Who has come to the foot of the stairs.)* Me?

HAYLEY. Yes, of course you. *(She links arms with him.)* You've been through purgatory. Now it's time to visit paradise.

HOPKINS. For what we are about to receive, may the Lord make us truly thankful.

*(They exit U.L. arm in arm. ABDUL is waving his hand with a piece of paper in it.)*

MAUREEN. He's trying to tell us something.

TERRI. *(Takes the piece of paper.)* Why it's a check. Brian, it's a certified check, payable to us for — for — it's a hundred thousand dollars more than the asking price.

MAJOR. *(Enters from room 8, followed by ASHLEY.)* I say old chap. I heard somebody shout, is everything alright?

*(ABDUL raises himself up, and looks U.L. toward the MAJOR with outstretched arms.)*

**(The curtain falls.)**

## COSTUME PLOT

HOPKINS:
White overalls
T-shirt
Baseball cap
Tool belt
Tennis shoes
Socks
Dark suit
Black shirt/clerical collar
Dress shoes and socks
Boxers

TERRI CODY:
Light-weight cotton skirt
Blouse
White sandals
Linen suit
Turquoise silk blouse
Hose
High heel shoes
Hat
Jewelry

BRIAN CODY:
Cotton pants
Tropical pants
Loafers
Casual shoes
Socks

MAJOR PONSENBY:
Tan pants
White military-style shirt
Dress shoes and socks
T-shirt with medal ribbons, etc.
White boxers with Union Jack
Long flowing Arab robe
Burnoose

MAUREEN:
Shorts
T-shirt
Black dress
White apron
Hose and high heels
Wig
Tailored jacket and skirt
White blouse
Black lace teddy
Garter belt and stockings

SAM LEWIS:
Business suit
Shirt
Tie
Socks
Dress shoes
T-shirt
Boxers

HAYLEY HARRINGTON:
Summer dress
Bolero jacket
High heel shoes
Silk robe
Sheet

ASHLEY:
Light- weight summer suit
Blouse
High heel shoes
Jewelry
Floral lace teddy

DOROTHY LEWIS:
Dark drab suit
Flat shoes
Hat
Bloomers
Corset
Undershirt

THE FALLEN FIGURE
OF ABDUL EL HAJJ:
Long flowing Arab robe
Burnoose
Pants, shoes and socks *(all identical to those worn by the Major)*

## FURNITURE AND PROPERTY LIST

### Act 1: On Stage

Key racks with keys
Booking charts
Call bell
Telephone (counter)
Check-in forms
Two low-backed easy chairs
Small table
Stand up ashtray with bottle inside
Newel post with removable knob — and bottle with two shot glasses inside
Painting hinged with bottle inside
Still life painting with removable bottle
Hanging light fixture with wrist strap
Double bed — bedspread, pillows, etc.
Two bedside tables with lamps
Bedside telephone
Semi-circular table
Vase of flowers — bottle inside
"Do Not Disturb" sign (Room 7)
Writing pad (counter)

### Act 1: Off Stage
Brian's shoes (Terri)
Bucket and mop (Maureen)
Plunger (Hopkins)
Toolbox containing: whiskey glass,
    flask with ice cubes, tablecloth
    (Hopkins)
Step ladder (Major)
Trick light bulb (Brian)
Maureen's clothes (Terri)
Screwdriver (Major)
Clothes on a hanger (Maureen)
Index cards (Maureen)
Suitcase (Sam)
Suitcase (Ashley)
Suitcase (Abdul)
Ice bucket (Maureen)
Bible — cut out with bottle inside
    (Hopkins)
Tray with cups and saucers
    (Maureen)
Suitcase (Hayley)
Clothes on hangers (Hayley)
Two trays with two open
    champagne bottles in ice
    buckets and seven glasses
    (Maureen)

### Act 2: Off Stage
Bundle of underwear (Ashley)
Dress on hanger (Ashley)
Tray — champagne — ice
    bucket — two glasses (Sam)
Bra (Abdul)
Sheet (Hayley)
Tool box (Hopkins)
Dress (Terri)
Briefcase (Sam)
Suitcase (Hayley)
Towel (Maureen)
Suitcase (Dorothy)
Tray with two drinks (Maureen)
Bundle of clothes including a
    black lace bra (Maureen)

### Personal
Handkerchief (Hopkins)
Business card (Sam)
Check (Abdul)

## AUTHOR'S NOTES

The construction of the staircase should be such that a double for Abdul can be concealed on the landing and switch with him in the middle of the fall. This can be achieved by having Abdul fall out of sight for a split second before continuing to fall without missing a beat. Both actors can enter or leave by means of an escape R. of the landing. At the final curtain I suggest that the actor playing the Major change once again to the fallen figure of Abdul before the curtain rises for the curtain call.

The Hanging light should have a lantern-type fixture so as to be able to conceal a wrist loop from which Brian can hang free of the ladder.

The still life picture should contain a real bottle of wine which is lifted out of the picture by Hopkins.

# HOTBED HOTEL SCENIC DESIGN

## Works by
## Michael Parker...

## The Amorous Ambassador

## Hotbed Hotel

## The Lone Star Love Potion

## Never Kiss a Naughty Nanny

## The Sensuous Senator

## There's a Burglar in My Bed

## Who's in Bed with the Butler

## Whose Wives Are They Anyway?

(with Susan Parker)

## Sex Please We're Sixty!

## Sin, Sex, and the C.I.A.

## What is Susan's Secret?

Please visit our website **samuelfrench.com** for complete
descriptions and licensing information.